Dawn

Other books by
Ann M. Martin

Leo the Magnificat
Rachel Parker, Kindergarten Show-off
Eleven Kids, One Summer
Ma and Pa Dracula
Yours Turly, Shirley
Ten Kids, No Pets
Slam Book
Just a Summer Romance
Missing Since Monday
With You and Without You
Me and Katie (the Pest)
Stage Fright
Inside Out
Bummer Summer

THE KIDS IN MS. COLMAN'S CLASS series
BABY-SITTERS LITTLE SISTER series
THE BABY-SITTERS CLUB mysteries
THE BABY-SITTERS CLUB series
CALIFORNIA DIARIES series

California

Dawn

Ann M. Martin

SCHOLASTIC INC.
New York Toronto London Auckland Sydney

For Laura

ISBN 0-590-29835-6

10 9 8 7 6 5 4 3 2   0 1/0

Printed in the U.S.A   40

First Scholastic printing, August 1997

Friday afternoon 9 / 26

Well, here I am, starting another new journal. This is my second since school began, and it isn't even October yet. It turns out that this is an appropriate day to start a new journal, since I feel like one part of my life has ended (way too abruptly), and a new and very scary one has suddenly begun. But the new, scary part didn't start until the end of school, so I'll get to that in a minute. I want to back up first and record yesterday, which was when everything _really_ began. It started off normally. There was no sign of what was to come — no dark skies or weird violin music.

I woke up thinking about friends — my friends, and friends in general. Sometimes I just don't understand friends. Like, why do they have to change all the time? Something is going on with every single one of my good friends, and I don't like any of it. They're probably writing about me right now in their journals. They're saying that Dawn Schafer should just settle down and not get so distracted by school. Well, I can't help getting distracted. I mean, just this morning, for instance, I was thinking about what I don't like about eighth grade. It's really been bothering me. Okay, so Vista is divided into those three main buildings. The biggest one is the high school building for grades nine, ten, eleven, and twelve. The middle-sized one is for preschool through grade four, and the smallest one is mine, the middle school building, for grades five through eight. Well, my building is soooo crowded this year. Suddenly there isn't enough space for us all. There are about a thousand kids in each class, and there aren't even enough rooms for us. My math class is held in the gym — on Tuesdays and Fridays. On the other days it's held in the back of the auditorium, while an English class meets in the front. It's a mess and I hate it. No wonder I'm distracted by school. I can't concentrate or settle down.

See? Just thinking about school made me get off track. I was talking about my friends, then ... poof.

Maybe — _maybe_ — what was announced

today will be for the better. But I'm not holding my breath.

Anyway . . . back to yesterday morning.

As always, I walked to Vista with Sunny and Maggie. I left crabby Jeff behind, glad he was going to walk to school with his dorky friends. First I went next door and stood outside Sunny's house. In the old days I used to barge up the walk to her front door and ring the bell. Sometimes I'd even go inside without ringing. I knew Sunny and her parents would just be eating their breakfast. Now I never know what to do. Or at any rate, I don't know what to do during those times Mrs. Winslow is home from the hospital. Like, if I ring the bell will I wake her up? Do they want me to come in or do they need as much private family time as they can get?

I was standing at the bottom of the front stoop, feeling like a jerk, when the door burst open and Sunny barreled outside.

"Okay, let's go," she said.

I noticed she was holding a bag of granola. "Didn't you eat breakfast?" I asked her. "You can eat first. We don't have to rush."

"That's okay. I'll eat on the way to school. Mom's having a horrible morning. She's on chemo again and the drugs are making her sick."

At first I didn't say anything. I was thinking that if my mom were really sick, I'd want to stay at home with her. Or at least not flee the house early in order to get away from her. Then I realized maybe that wasn't true. I mean, how do I know how I would react if Mom had lung cancer? Maybe I would do just what Sunny has been doing lately.

Sunny was practically running down the sidewalk.

"Hey, wait!" I called. "Slow down."

Sunny slowed down. A little.

We turned a corner. I always feel the exact same way when I reach the end of our street and make that left onto Palm Boulevard. Like I've stepped onto a movie set or something. Maybe it's because Palm is the unofficial divider of my middle-class neighborhood and Maggie's definitely-not-middle-class neighborhood. All those swimming pools and tennis courts. I feel uncomfortable. Like I shouldn't even be looking down those streets.

Yikes. My hand is getting tired. More later.

Friday, later on, 9/26

Vista may seem like a big mess to me right now, but there are some things I like about it very much. The journal idea is one of the best things about Vista. I bet most of the students are like me and would keep journals even if the teachers didn't require it. At least they would keep them by the time they left Vista's elementary building and moved into the middle school building. It seems to me that just around that time, around fifth and sixth grade, everything begins to happen. Suddenly life gets so complicated. I suppose that life always gets more complicated. I mean, the older you are, the more complicated it is. In kindergarten, for example, what do you have to worry about except whether your friend will share her crayons with you. It seems like such a big deal at the time. Then by third grade you have to worry about whether William Barton is going to kiss you on the playground, and it's enough to make you fake a stomachache so you can stay home from school. But you have no idea what's coming, what you'll be up against when you're ten, twelve, thirteen. For me, things heated up until they spun out of control when I was twelve. That was the year Mom and Dad got divorced, and Mom moved Jeff and me all the way across the country to Connecticut. We had to say good-bye to California, to Vista, to everyone and everything. I thought my heart would break when I had to say good-bye to Sunny. I truly didn't know how to say good-bye to my best friend. Then Connecticut turned out to be cool, figuratively and literally. I made friends, Mom got remarried, and I acquired a stepfather and a stepsister, who already happened to be my Connecticut best friend. Then Jeff decided to move back to California, then I did too, and then Dad married Carol. Not exactly in that order. The point is that there was a _lot_ (a very huge IMMENSE lot) going on in my life, and through it all I kept my journals. All right, I admit I didn't write in them quite as much when I went to Stoneybrook Middle School, where journal-keeping was not required (like it is at Vista, starting in kindergarten, when you can barely write, and continuing until the day you graduate from twelfth grade). I know why the teachers make us keep these journals, apart from the fact that this activity is a healthy habit, a creative outlet, good writing practice, and all that. The teachers never say so, but (since they were all kids themselves once) I bet they remember what it's like to be _consumed_ by feelings and to need an outlet for them. Or maybe that's not a kid thing. Maybe it's just a human thing. Anyway, when I start to feel eaten up, or even when I'm just feeling chatty, which is pretty often, I like to turn to my current journal. (This one is #22.)

Friday evening 9/26

Maggie was waiting for Sunny and me on her corner. I thought she looked like she'd been crying. But all she said when she saw us was, "Hi, you guys. How's your mother, Sunny?"

"Don't ask."

"Oh. Sorry."

Sunny looked at Maggie. Then she looked at her a bit harder. "No, I'm sorry," she said gently. "What's wrong, Maggie?"

"Nothing." But Maggie was definitely trying not to cry.

"Is it your mom again?" asked Sunny.

"Or your dad?" I suggested.

"Not really. I just, um... I needed more time to study for our math quiz. I didn't plan very well, I guess. I don't think I can get an A on the quiz now."

I don't know if that's really what was wrong. It might have been. Maggie's awfully hard on herself when it comes to school. Actually when it comes to just about anything. Miss Perfection. She used to be rebellious and do things like dye her hair green, which I kind of admired. Now she's made this turnaround, and she tries to control everything. And excel at everything.

Sunny and I let the subject drop. "How's Curtis?" Sunny finally asked. She was smiling.

The mention of Curtis made Maggie smile too. "Good!" she replied. "Mom didn't really like having to go out and get a prescription for amoxicillin for a kitten, but it was worth it. I had to pay her back. I don't care, though. His paw healed up."

"Are your parents going to let you keep him?"

"No, but it doesn't matter. I just want to fix him up, then find a good home for him."

We turned off of Palm, walked two more blocks, turned again, and there was Vista.

"You know, it even looks more crowded," I said. "Doesn't it?"

The front lawn was crawling with kids.

"It's morning," said Sunny, already impatient with me. "Of course it's crowded. Everyone's arriving. All the buses just got here."

"But it's more crowded than usual," I replied.

"She's right," said Maggie. "Well, a lot of kids do switch to Vista in seventh or eighth grade so they can go to the high school, since it's so good."

"Why'd they let so many in this year?" I grumbled.

"Hi! Hi, guys!" we heard someone call then.

It was Jill, of course. She was hopping off of her bus and running across the lawn toward us.

"Oh, please. What is she wearing?" Sunny said under her breath.

"She must have found her first-grade things," Maggie whispered. "I wonder how she got them to fit."

Jill was wearing a sweatshirt with a

huge pink unicorn on the front. The unicorn's horn (why aren't unicorns called unihorns?) was sparkly gold, and the unicorn was standing on a powder blue cloud that was made of some puffy material. On Jill's feet were pink sneakers, and on the toe of each sneaker was a pony with an actual tail hanging over the side of the shoe.

"Hi," we called back to Jill.

No one said anything about Jill's shirt or shoes, which I thought was commendable of us. Then I realized that Jill _wanted_ us to comment. And so her face fell when Sunny looked beyond her and said, "Well, I guess we have to go in."

I glanced at my watch. "Yeah. The bell is going to ring any minute. Come on, you guys."

Later Friday evening 9 / 26
My friends thought I found school distracting before, but that was nothing. Yesterday was out of control. Maggie and

Jill and Sunny and I walked across the lawn, through the main entrance, outside again into the courtyard, and then into the middle school building. Really, I felt like our building was just oozing kids. I wouldn't have been surprised to see them seeping out of windows or through cracks around doors like mold or bacteria.

In my homeroom we were short two chairs, so Brent and Max sat on a windowsill. It turned out that the chairs had been taken by the teacher next door who suddenly had two new kids in her class.

"What is going on?" I whispered to Tray Farmer, who sits next to me and knows everything. (Well, he has an answer for everything, anyway. I think he makes some stuff up, but it always sounds good.)

"It's the current surge in eighth-grade enrollment," he replied, and I noticed that little tic by his left eye.

"I guess, but why?"

"Vista is an excellent private school, Dawn," he said. "Progressive yet demanding. Challenging yet accepting of a student's special needs and/or gifts."

I looked around to see where Tray was hiding the Vista brochure. It must have been there somewhere.

"An atmosphere of — "

"I know, I know." I cut him off. "I mean, why are there so many _more_ eighth-graders this year?"

This was one question for which Tray had no answer. At least not a quick one. His face was still screwed into a frown when the bell rang and homeroom began.

Out in the hallway after homeroom, I squeezed my way through the halls. I am not exaggerating when I say "squeezed." At one point I really did have to ooze between two bunches of kids in order to go past them. I felt like toothpaste in a tube. At the end of the hall, I caught sight of Sunny. She saw me. But we couldn't reach each other, so she just raised her fist in the air and called out, "Rulers!"

"Rulers!" I shouted back.

Sunny and Maggie and Jill and I have waited for years to be able to do that. As eighth-graders we are the Rulers of the middle school building. It's a nice position to be in. I wonder why the seniors don't bother to call themselves Rulers of the high school. Oh, well. I'd intended to enjoy my status this year. I'd earned it.

                       Saturday morning 9/27
    Okay, so I ran out of steam last night and never got around to writing about what happened in school. Or maybe I was afraid to write about it — as if putting the words on paper would make it seem even more real (and horrible). But there's no point in delaying any longer. So here goes.
    At the very end of school on Thursday, Mr. Dean's voice came over the loudspeaker, and he said, "Attention, all eighth-graders. Please report to the main auditorium tomorrow morning at 9:30 for an assembly with the students in grades nine through twelve. Thank you for your time." (He's always formal like that.)
    An assembly for us eighth-graders

with the _high_ school kids? We never do things with the high school kids. And why just the eighth-graders? Why not the rest of the middle-schoolers? That was weird.

Well, guess what. What happened at the assembly was beyond weird. It was unbelievable. And scary. At 9:30 all us eighth-graders were excused from our classes, and we left the middle school building and walked to the auditorium. I met Sunny, Maggie, and Jill at the entrance to the auditorium. Sunny and Maggie and I tried hard to look like we weren't actually _with_ Jill, since she was wearing this sweatshirt with huge crayons painted on the front. You could tell she thought it was cute, but _really_. Anyway, the four of us walked into the auditorium, and suddenly I felt the way I did at my very first assembly at Vista. I was a kindergartner then, and the assembly was for all the kids in the lower grades, so there I was with the fourth-graders. They looked like giants to me, and I felt like a pea.

That is exactly the way I felt with the high school kids. I'd like to think I am just as cool and just as grown-up as they are. But, well, I got a good look at them. Some of the guys have to shave. And some of them must be six feet tall. I mean real adult men. And the senior girls? Real adult women. Who have huge chests and wear lots of makeup. And, I don't know, I just felt like they were way more than four or five years older than me.

Let me put it this way. Since some of the seniors are eighteen already, we are talking about kids who can drive and vote. Among other things. I looked at this one enormous guy who could practically have been my father. Then I looked at Jill in her crayon sweatshirt. My heart began to pound — and I didn't even know what the assembly was going to be about.

Believe me, we found out soon enough.

This was the announcement: Because the middle school has become overcrowded this year (due to the current surge in eighth-grade enrollment, just like Tray had said), the eighth-graders are going to move to the high school building. The middle school building at Vista will now be for grades five, six, and seven. The high school building will be for grades eight, nine, ten, eleven, and twelve.

Maggie, Sunny, Jill, and I are in high school.

Saturday afternoon 9/27

We're in high school.

I just cannot believe it.

Over the weekend, things will be moved around in the high school building to make room for us eighth-graders. And on Monday morning, we will report to the high school.

The high school.

Unthinkable.

"We won't be the Rulers anymore," I said sadly to my friends as we walked out of the assembly.

I might add here that us eighth-graders did not look like the only ones in shock. The high school kids looked pretty shocked, too. And no wonder. A big bunch of babies were about to join their ranks. I'm sure that's what they thought as they looked around and saw things like crayon sweatshirts. (And Peg, this other friend of Jill's, was actually carrying a troll doll. It was sticking out of her puppy backpack.)

"Forget being the Rulers. We're going to be going to school with kids like that guy," whispered Maggie. She was pointing to this humongous guy with a crew cut who was wearing fatigues and dangling a ring of car keys. He was walking along with his arm slipped through the arm of a girl in a dress so tight you could almost see her pores through it. You could certainly see her D-cup breasts.

Jill began to giggle. "He looks like — " she started to say.

"Shut up. He'll hear you." Sunny cut her off.

Jill clamped her mouth shut. She looked wounded and embarrassed. I felt sorry for her. But not sorry enough to say anything.

The four of us kept quiet until we were outside and on our way back to the middle school building.

"What do we know about high school?" Jill finally asked.

"Well, we were going to be over there next year anyway," replied Sunny, "so what's the big deal?"

"I don't know," mumbled Jill.

We were quiet again. Then Sunny said, "Well, _I'm_ excited. This is going to be cool. It's the big time, you guys. We'll get a whole extra year of parties, dates with older guys, all the good stuff. I feel like we've been in middle school forever."

"I _like_ middle school," said Jill.

She sounded as if she might cry. But the only thing anyone said then was, "I don't really care what we do." (That was Maggie.) "I mean, what's the big deal? We'll still be at Vista. Does it matter what building we're in? Anyway, I will just be _so_ glad not to be squished and squeezed and bumped all the time."

At the exact moment that Maggie said that, a sixth-grade boy crashed into her from behind. He had lost control when a surge of kids leaving the middle school building knocked him off his feet. He could not understand why this caused Maggie and Sunny and me to start laughing hysterically.

Sunday night 9/28

Well, as my dad would say, "When it rains, it pours." Maybe I should have been expecting more shocking news, but I just wasn't. That bombshell about school seemed like enough to deal with. However, something else was in store. Dad dropped his own bombshell at dinner tonight.

Everything had started off so peacefully. Mrs. Bruen had returned to work early this afternoon. I like when she comes in on Sunday. I think she knew I was upset about the high school news, so while I was starting my homework and worrying about tomorrow, she brought a cup of herbal tea to my room. It was peppermint.

"Very soothing," said Mrs. Bruen.

Occasionally I wish Dad had married

Mrs. Bruen instead of Carol, even though I know that's entirely out of the question. I mean, Mrs. Bruen is, like, sixty, about twenty years older than Dad. Oh, well. At least she's our housekeeper. That means she's here five or six days a week. Plus, she's an excellent cook, which makes up for Carol.

Anyway, the peppermint tea _was_ soothing. By the time I sat down to dinner with Dad and Jeff and Carol, my homework half done, I felt a lot calmer. And so we were just eating away at our salad and pasta when Dad cleared his throat. The throat clearing was followed by a glance around the table, but even before the glance I sensed bad news.

Sure enough.

"Well," said Dad.

"What," said Jeff. Just like that. It wasn't even a question. Jeff knew as well as I did that we weren't going to like whatever Dad had to say. Parents can be so transparent.

"I'm going on a business trip," said Dad.

Oh. That didn't seem so bad.

"For ten days," Dad added.

"Ten days?" I cried.

"Starting when?" asked Carol.

"Where are you going?" asked Jeff. "Someplace good? Can I go with you?" He paused. "You're not going to, say, Florida, are you?"

Dad looked overwhelmed, but he was smiling. "It's just another business trip, Dawn," he said. "I've been traveling a lot lately."

"I know. But only for a day or two. Not ten days."

"When do you leave?" asked Carol.

"Tomorrow."

"Tomorrow?" I said in dismay.

"Well, tomorrow evening. After work. Why?"

"Tomorrow is the first day we'll be in the high school building," I replied. "I was hoping you'd be around for awhile. I mean, that'll be such a big change. I just wanted, I don't know, moral support."

"I'll be here," said Carol.

"I know." How could I tell her that was not the same thing?

"Where are you going, Dad?" Jeff asked again.

"Toledo. In Ohio," Dad added when the city didn't seem to register with Jeff.

"Oh." Total boredom. Jeff returned to his pasta.

"Hey, come on, you guys. We'll have fun," Carol said to Jeff and me. "We'll go out to dinner one night. And to the beach on Saturday."

"Can we go to the Arnold Schwarzenegger movie?" asked Jeff, sensing an opportunity. "And then go bowling?"

"Sure, why not?" said Carol.

Admittedly, these things sounded kind of fun. Even the movie. But I'm mad. How can Dad go off and abandon me at this time in my life? It's not fair.

Later Sunday night 9 / 28

Carol and I had another fight tonight. Actually, it wasn't a fight. That's too strong a word. And it wasn't a disagreement because we didn't disagree about anything. I

don't know what you'd call it, but this is
what happened: I'd just gotten off the
phone with Sunny. She'd been talking to me
about her mother, who's back in the hospital.
And she was upset. Now, I needed to ask
someone about something Sunny said about
her mom's treatment, and I needed to talk
to a woman. So I went to Carol and I
asked her what "sterile" means. First Carol
blushed, then she started to giggle. I said,
"Carol, this is serious." Carol couldn't stop
giggling. I don't know why, now that I've
looked up sterile in the dictionary and found
out what it means. Carol is so immature.
I'd like to confide in her, but sometimes I
just can't.

Later

I was just thinking. All my friends
seem to be changing. Ever since Sunny's
mom got cancer, Sunny has seemed a
little...wild or something. She takes risks.
She's daring. And she's not so interested in

the stuff we used to do together. She's especially not interested in baby-sitting.

And all Maggie cares about these days are her animals and trying to be perfect. She has to be the perfect everything. Perfect student, perfect daughter, perfect sister, perfect friend. Everything in her life is scheduled and controlled. Doesn't she know she'll never please her parents? She's a misfit in her own family. But she doesn't talk about it much.

Then there's Jill. Actually, Jill isn't changing, at least not in comparison to the rest of us. She still seems more like a seventh-grader (a _young_ seventh-grader) than an eighth-grader. I am tired of oohing and ahhing over her teddy bear collection.

We seem like such a different group of friends than we used to be. I'm not sure I like this.

Monday 9 / 29

I am writing this during study hall on my first day as a high school student. I feel like I'm the new kid in a whole new school, not just at Vista, where I've been going to school practically all my life. I mean, this is JUST SO WEIRD.

Plus, and this is even weirder, I'm scared.

Yes. Really scared.

The high school building feels so big. And it is a little bigger than the middle school building, but not _that_ much bigger. Maybe it's because it isn't overcrowded. There's more space, and that makes everything feel bigger.

So right now I'm in a study hall. In this building, they have an actual room just for study hall. It's like a giant classroom with some reference books in case you need them.

Get this. I do not know one single other person in the room. I think I recognize a few other eighth-graders. And one of them might be named Amelia or Amalia or something. She's new this year. Then there are all these older kids. That huge guy with the crew cut and the fatigues is here. He's sitting at a table with a different girl, though. I can't even look at him.

The one person I do look at sometimes is this guy who held the door open for me when I came into the room. He's definitely one of the older kids, and he is definitely very nice. He doesn't look particularly cool, but everyone seems to know him. Kids (girls mostly, it looks like) want to sit at his table. Right now he's sitting with another guy and two girls, and they're studying, but not in a nerdy way.

Oh. My. God.

The study hall monitor (a teacher, I can't remember his name) just left the room for a minute, and the big, scary guy and the girl started making out. They didn't even move to the back of the room. They are just sitting in their chairs (well, they moved them closer together, obviously) and they are ALL OVER EACH OTHER. The guy has lipstick on his cheek. I have never seen anything like this at close range.

I'm staring, and I can't help myself.

There is an incredible amount of slobber.
Oh, well, now here comes

Monday afternoon 9 / 29

When that study hall monitor came back,
all hell broke loose. No, that's an
exaggeration. But what happened was hostile.
Very, very quietly hostile. The monitor came
back (I still can't remember his name),
and he was furious, and he said, "Dex, how
many times have I spoken to you about
this?" (Is the big, scary guy's name
Dexter? Now that's funny.) Dex's face turned
red, but it was an angry red, not an
embarrassed red. And I could tell the
teacher was afraid of him ... afraid of him.

Oh, I have so much more to say. I
mean, this was the first day of high school
(when you think about it) and I didn't
even start at the beginning. I jumped into
the middle of the morning and then I got
all caught up in the study hall incident. I
want to go back to the beginning of the day
and not get so bogged down by details.

When I got up this morning I was so nervous I almost barfed. Really. I had horrible butterflies in my stomach. The first thing I thought about was all those big kids we'd seen last week. Then I spent about half an hour choosing an outfit, and in the end I wore... jeans and a T-shirt. How original.

I met Sunny and Maggie as usual. Sunny looked nervous but excited, and even a little proud. Maggie was biting her nails. The first thing she said to us was, "Do you guys know what hazing is?"

"Hazing?" Sunny repeated.

"I guess," I replied. "Why?"

"Do you think the upperclassmen are going to do anything to us?" Maggie asked, thumbnail in her mouth.

"Well —" I started to say.

"Because you know they get to haze the freshmen on the first day of school. But the first day of school is over, and we aren't freshmen. Technically."

"We're subfreshmen," said Sunny. "Sort of like bacteria."

"I wonder what they're going to do to us," I said.

As it turned out, not much.

You know what? I'm on a roll, but my hand is about to fall off from so much writing. Plus, I have a lot of homework. I have to stop now. I'll pick up later.

When I said "later," I meant later that day, not 28 hours later. But here it is, Tuesday night. I haven't even finished my homework. Still, I really need my journal. I have so much to say.

Okay, there were a few little hazing incidents, but not many. The teachers had put out the word that it was _not_ the first day of school, that classes were in full swing, and that basically this was supposed to be just another day. So we were kind of off the hook.

One eighth-grader got lipsticked. The funny thing is that on the first day of school, the upperclassmen get to mark the letter F on the foreheads of the freshmen with red lipstick, but since we aren't exactly freshmen, this guy put an 8 on the kid's forehead.

Another kid's wallet was taken during gym class. (That may or may not have been hazing.) Two girls, at separate times, were given directions to the boys' locker room when they asked where the library was. Stuff like that. So all in all, we made it through our first day of high school without much of anything happening. Mostly, I just kept noticing the older kids, now that I could see them up close, I mean. I felt like I was a naturalist in the wild and for years I'd been studying the gorillas from afar. But now, suddenly, I was living among them.

"There are some very cute guys," Maggie said at the end of that first day. Her fingernails were bitten down to little nubs, but otherwise she looked pretty good. "I mean, some very cute _older_ guys. Do any of you know who Justin Randall is?" Her eyes took on this faraway look.

"No," said Jill.

"_Is_ he a junior?" I asked.

"Yes, he is," said Sunny. "And Maggie,

he's already taken. Every girl in school has a crush on him. Pick someone easier."

Maggie just shrugged. Then grinned. Sunny and I grinned back. Maggie's smile was contagious.

Except to Jill, who must have developed an immunity.

"What's wrong?" I asked her.

It was Jill's turn to shrug. But, unlike Maggie, she looked miserable.

"Well, anyway, we all made it," I said cheerfully.

Day One was over.

Later Tuesday night 9/30

Day One was over at school, but not at home.

Dad returned from the office at about four and packed two suitcases. Carol came home at 4:30, which meant she had left her office early. The next hour was hectic. Mrs. Bruen was still there, trying to finish making dinner before she left for the evening. I was trying to tell Dad about school, Jeff was trying to tell him about a problem with his soccer coach, Carol was trying to ask him questions about the next ten days, and Dad was trying to _tell_ all of us about the next ten days but kept being interrupted by his boss, who phoned him four times.

Carol seemed really nervous about something. She wanted to drive Dad to the airport by herself, but Jeff and I insisted on coming along, so Dad said we could. Carol did not look happy. Still, after Dad's plane had taken off, she turned to Jeff and me, smiling, and said we were going to have a great ten days together. I tried to feel convinced.

Wednesday afternoon 10/1
What happened today was so embarrassing I can barely bring myself to write about it. Just thinking about it now makes me flush. Honest. I can feel my

cheeks getting hot. And the thing is, it really didn't have to blow up into such an incident. Mandy Richards is a pain in the butt.

Okay, all us eighth-graders have new lockers, right? We're in the new building, so of course we do. And the new building (new to us, I mean) is confusing. I haven't quite figured it out yet. Anyway, my new locker number is 106B. It's number 106 in the B wing. It's a pretty good locker. I haven't had any trouble opening it. But yesterday after lunch I just could not get it open. I kept turning the dial and nothing would happen. Finally I found the piece of paper from the main office with my combination on it. I checked it. I was using the right combination. So I tried it again. Nothing.

I tried it for like the eighth time.

Nothing.

And then I whammed it with my fist. Sometimes that would unstick my old locker. It didn't unstick this one. So I whammed it two more times and then I kicked it.

"_Excuse_ me," said this really snitty voice from behind me.

I turned around. A girl was standing there. She looked like a junior or maybe a senior.

"Oh. Sorry I was making so much noise," I said.

"Me too," she said. "Since you're making it on _my_ locker."

"_Your_ locker?"

The girl rolled her eyes. Then she shoved me aside.

"Mandy?" someone called. Two other girls were hurrying toward us. They stopped at the locker.

"This _jerk_," said Mandy, pointing at me, "was trying to break into my locker. Can you believe it?"

"I was not trying to break in!" I exclaimed. "I thought it was my locker. Isn't it number 106B?"

"No. It is not 106B," said Mandy. "It is 106D."

I peered at the faded number on the locker. Sure enough.

"What an actress," said one of the other girls. Then she turned to Mandy. "See if she got anything. Is anything missing?"

Mandy wrestled the door open. "No."
She paused. Then she glared at me. "But
thanks a lot for breaking my mirror."

I could see where Mandy had fastened
a makeup mirror to the inside of her door.
(A fancy nameplate over the mirror said
MANDY RICHARDS, which is how I know her
name.) My whamming had caused the
mirror to fall off of its nail. Now it lay on
the floor of the locker in a million pieces.

"Oops," I said.

The three girls were looking at me like
I had three heads. I mean, really, they
were so condescending and snotty.

"I'll buy you another mirror," I said
quickly. "Here." I opened my purse to get
out some money. And inside (this is the
part I can hardly bear to think about) I
found a fuzzy toy puppy. A note was
attached to its tail. It could only have been
from Jill. Some sort of surprise she'd
planted for me.

"What is that?" exclaimed Mandy.

"Oh, it's nothing."

Mandy took the puppy out of my purse

and held it between her thumb and forefinger. Her friends started to laugh.

"No need to pay for the mirror," said Mandy. "I'll take this instead."

"You —" I started to say. I paused. "Don't you _ever_ put your hand in my purse again. That is private."

Mandy frowned. Then she stepped forward, but suddenly one of her friends grabbed her and jerked her back.

"Don't, Mandy," she said.

And Mandy didn't do whatever it was she'd started to do, but her eyes were flashing. Luckily, the other girl distracted her. She pulled the note off the tail, opened it, and read it aloud. "'Here is a little good-luck friend for you,'" she read. She glanced at Mandy. "A _good-luck_ friend?" She looked back at the note. "'Keep it with you always. Your puppy pal, Jill.'"

Suddenly, I couldn't take it anymore. I turned and ran down the hall. Believe me, I have truly _never_ been _so_ embarrassed. Not in my whole life.

Of course, since then I've seen Mandy

and her friends about a hundred times, and they always snicker and call me Puppy Pal. (Mandy's snicker is accompanied by those flashing eyes of hers.)

I think I am going to kill them. After that, I will kill Jill.

Later Wednesday night 10/1

At last a moment of peace. I think I'm the only one who's awake in our house right now. Jeff went to bed almost two hours ago, and Carol has been in her room for about an hour. I just saw the light disappear from the crack under her door. She might be watching TV in bed, but I don't think so. Carol was exhausted tonight. Plus, she kept harping on me about homework, which I don't have. But she didn't believe me. "It's the beginning of the year," she said. "You should have a ton of homework right now."

The thing is, she was right. But the teachers haven't been giving us much work. I think they've been crazed this year, spending all their time dealing with new students. But did I say this to Carol? No, I just got all defensive, like I usually do with her. I said, "If I had homework, don't you think I'd be doing it?"

"Dawn," she said warningly.

"You're always picking on me." (Carol just looked at me.) "Well, you are!"

"I am *not* picking," Carol said in this staccato voice. And then she marched into her room. She doesn't understand me, and I don't understand her.

Thursday afternoon 10/2

It's a quiet time, and I'm home alone. Carol and Jeff and Mrs. Bruen are all out together. Carol decided Jeff needs new school clothes, and instead of being thrilled at the prospect of shopping, Jeff threw a fit. He said he doesn't need anything new, that all his ripped jeans and too-tight shirts are fine. Now, it's true that you can wear just about anything you want at Vista, but honestly, Jeff looks awfully raggedy some days. Anyway, he said Carol has no idea what fifth—grade boys wear, which is probably also true, so he insisted that Mrs. Bruen go along, since she's known him for so long. I think the whole thing is a mistake.

Wait — the phone is ring

The phone call was from Mary Anne. I miss my stepsister, but you know what? This is a terrible thing to write. However, since no one but me ever reads my journals I know I can say it safely — I don't miss Mary Anne or my other Connecticut friends as much as I thought I would. I mean, I love them and I miss them and everything, and I'm glad the custody arrangements are for Mom to have Jeff and me in Connecticut for vacations and in the summer. But my friends do seem far away, as far as Stoneybrook is from Palo City.

Well, I was going to continue writing but Jeff and Carol and Mrs. Bruen just came back. They haven't even been gone an hour. This is not a good sign.

Thursday night 10 / 2

Boy, did Jeff make a scene this afternoon. He probably already wrote about it in his journal. And I have a pretty good idea what his entry looks like. Jeff is not very concerned with privacy. He leaves his journals everywhere. Once he saw me reading his (he had left it open right out on the coffee table in the living room), and he didn't even care. It was full of paragraphs like this:

I HATE DAWN SHE IS SO STUPID. I DO NOT EVEN WANT TO PLAY WITH HER OR HER STUPID FREINDS WHO NEEDS SISTERS. I WISH I WAS A ONLY CHILD

Anyway, I still do not know exactly what went on during the shopping trip, only that a total of one pair of tube socks was purchased. And then everyone came home in a foul mood. I could have asked what happened and someone would have told me, but I didn't really want to stir things up again. Besides, I can figure out what happened. A ten-year-old boy went clothes shopping with his stepmother and his housekeeper. Period.

I've been thinking. This afternoon Mary Anne asked me about the We ♥ Kids Club. And you know what? I'm a little confused about it, just like I'm a little confused about a lot of things right now. Okay. So the We ♥ Kids Club was never as organized a sitting business as the Baby-sitters Club is. We never held regular meetings or assigned officers like the BSC did when I was in Connecticut. We tried to do that once, and it lasted all of about three weeks. Sunny and Maggie and Jill and I simply decided that _baby-sitting_ is important to us, not officers and meetings. So in our haphazard way we got sitting jobs and we carried them out and we had fun. But lately we hardly meet at all. And you know something? Just like I don't miss Connecticut too much, I don't miss baby-sitting all that much either. I wonder why. And I wonder why my friends and I haven't been getting together so often. I mean, getting together for meetings. We get together to do other things all the time.

We're always hanging out. Not so much at Sunny's anymore because of her mom. And not so much at Jill's anymore because of ... well, because of Jill. Sometimes we hang out at my house or at Maggie's spread. More often we go to the movies, or shop, or stand around at the mall eyeing cute guys. (Girls always think boys so rudely check out girls. Well, girls check out guys all the time.) What is happening to baby-sitting and the We ♥ Kids Club?

You know what? Jill would love to continue the meetings and baby-sitting. That sort of goes along with her idea of hanging out, which includes cookie-baking and popcorn-making. However, Maggie

Oh, boy. My thoughts are all over the place. I'm giving myself a headache. I better go to bed. But what is happening to my friends?

Friday 10/3
Hmm. I hardly know what to say about what happened in school today. It's thrilling.

It's also really surprising, considering the Puppy Pal incident. Maybe the <u>nice</u> upperclassmen are behind it, not the mean ones.

    I just reread what I wrote and realize I'm not being clear, so let me start over and explain things better. Okay. When I got to school on Friday morning I went straight to my locker. (<u>My</u> locker. Not Mandy's. I'll never make that mistake again.) And sticking out of the vent at the top was a folded piece of paper. I opened it. It turned out to be an invitation to a party. This is what it looked like:

SHHH! It's a secret.

Come meet your fellow students and get acquainted.

The upperclassmen want to get to know you and a few others.

But only a <u>few</u> others —

<u>you</u>, the select few.

Food and drink served.

The fun starts at 10:00 on Saturday night.

Don't be early!

An address appeared at the bottom of the invitation. But no name. My first thought was that it was from Mandy and it was a joke. I mean, why would Puppy Pal be invited to a cool party put on by the upperclassmen for a select few eighth-graders?

But just then Sunny ran to me and grabbed me. She jumped up and down, squealing. "Look what I got! Look what I got!"

Sunny held out an invitation identical to mine.

Frowning, I held mine up for her to see.

"You got one too!" she cried.

"Yeah, but —"

"Hey! Hey, you guys! Look!" Maggie rushed to our sides, breathless. She held up another invitation.

"I —" I started to say.

Sunny couldn't contain herself. She cut me off, grinning. "I know for a fact that not everyone got one," she said. "Lucinda Dayton didn't get one, and neither did Dakota Wilde."

"Or Polly Guest," added Maggie.

"This is _so_ cool," cried Sunny. "It's the big time. A party given by the upperclassmen and they want to meet _us_."

"And the party doesn't even start until ten," added Maggie. "Extremely cool."

I started to feel more hopeful about the party.

Until lunchtime.

Friday afternoon 10/3

It was at lunch that I found out that Jill had gotten one of the invitations too. I waited until she had left the table to buy a carton of milk. Then I said, "If this party is for cool kids, how come Jill got invited?"

Sunny waved her hand. "Oh, they probably thought they _had_ to invite her. You know, because of us. They must have found out that we all hang out together and they didn't want to hurt Jill by leaving her out."

When I looked unconvinced, Maggie said, "You should hear who else was invited,

Dawn." And she began to reel off a list of the most popular eighth-graders.

"Really?" I said.

"Yup." Maggie nodded smugly.

Jill returned with her milk then.

"So?" Sunny said to us.

"So what?" I replied.

"So are we going?"

"Going to what?" asked Jill.

"The party," said Sunny.

"The one we just got the invitation to? Are you crazy?" said Jill. "We can't go to a party like that."

"Why not? We were invited," said Maggie.

"They are eleventh- and twelfth-graders!" cried Jill. "They're, like, four years older than us. Some of them are eighteen already."

"So what?" said Sunny. "I want to go. Besides, like Maggie said, they invited us. So they must want us at the party."

"It doesn't mean we belong there," said Jill. "Just think. They're going to be doing all sorts of stuff — "

"How do you know what they'll be doing?" asked Sunny.

"Come on, you guys," I said, interrupting them. "We don't have to decide this now. We have all today and tomorrow to think about it."

"Well, if we do go, we should probably bring something," Jill went on.

"What do you mean?" I asked.

"We can't show up at a party empty-handed. My mom says. We can bake cookies. Or make fudge."

"Fud—" Maggie started to say, an incredulous look on her face.

"We can _talk_ about it _later_," I said again. "End of discussion."

I snuck a look at Jill's face then. She seemed puzzled. She always seems puzzled lately. Ordinarily, that would have made me feel protective of her. But today I felt annoyed. And then I got mad at myself for feeling annoyed. What kind of friend am I?

Even later Friday afternoon 10/3

I wonder that a lot lately. What kind of friend am I? Actually, I think I mean what kind of person am I? What kind of friend, sister, stepsister, daughter, stepdaughter? I'm not always a very good person. I know that. I also know that most people are not "good" all the time, but that doesn't make me feel any better. I don't like being a bad friend, daughter, sister. But sometimes I can't help myself, and then I feel guilty.

Jill is driving me crazy.

Whoa. I just overheard the most amazing thing. I didn't mean to. Not exactly. I mean, I didn't intentionally eavesdrop. I just picked up the phone when it rang, and Carol picked it up at the same time on the downstairs extension, and when I heard the caller say, "This is Dr. Barnat," I somehow didn't manage to hang up the phone. Dr. Barnat is Carol's new gynecologist. And here she was calling Carol at 5:30. After office hours. Something was up. I really intended to hang up the phone, but at the last minute my hand wouldn't cooperate with my brain, so I was still on the extension when I heard Dr. Barnat say, "Well, your EPT was correct. You're pregnant. Roughly three weeks pregnant."

I did hang up the phone then, but only because I nearly dropped it. EPT. I know what that stands for. Early pregnancy test. Early pregnancy test.

Oh. My. God.

Carol is pregnant. I am going to be a big sister again. We are going to have a baby in the house.

Oh. My. GOD.

I am so amazed that I had to take a little break here and go get a drink of water and then throw some of that water on my face. I want to start making phone calls. I want to spread the news. You hear something like this and all of a sudden things that had recently seemed important (like deciding whether to go to the party) don't seem so important anymore. I know

I can't go calling people without talking to
Carol first, though.

Wait. She's off the phone. More later.

Well, I just do not understand Carol.
She isn't mad at me for eavesdropping. But

This is confusing. I'm going to start
over again.

Okay. It is now Friday night. Supper is
over. Jeff asked if we could eat on trays in
front of the TV, and Carol said that would
be all right. Now Jeff has gone to bed,
and Carol is puttering around her room.
We've already said good night. I'm alone,
thinking over what happened this afternoon.

After I hung up the phone, and after
I had recovered somewhat, I ran
downstairs. Carol was already off the phone.
She was sitting on a chair in the kitchen,
looking stunned.

"Carol?" I said. (She didn't answer.)
"Carol?"

"What? Oh, Dawn. I didn't hear you."

"Carol, I have to tell you something. I really didn't mean to do this, but I overheard part of your conversation with Dr. Barnat. I answered the phone when I heard it ring, and I picked it up just in time to hear Dr. Barnat say you're three weeks pregnant." Carol just looked at me. "I hung up then," I said. "Honest. I didn't mean to eavesdrop. I know it isn't—"

"Never mind," said Carol. "Don't worry about it."

I was so relieved not to be in trouble that my excitement about the baby bubbled over then. "Carol, you're going to have a baby!" I cried. "We're going to have a baby! I have a great name if it's a girl. Ashley. Isn't that a good name? Or better, we could spell it A—S—H—L—E—I—G—H."

Carol just sighed. "Honey, let's not get too excited right now."

"Why not? Is something wrong?" Maybe that's what the rest of the conversation had been about.

"No, no," said Carol quickly. "It's just that this isn't quite the way I'd

imagined this happening. I mean, with your
father away. I wanted to tell him the news
in person, and he's not going to be back
for six days. Plus, I wanted him to be the
first to know. So Dawn, you _have_ to keep
this a secret. Please. Please don't tell a soul.
Okay?"

    "Okay," I said slowly. "I promise."

    The more I thought about this later,
though, the more it didn't seem right. What's
the big deal about telling Dad in person?
I have a horrible feeling something else is
going on.

Saturday 10/4

    This morning Maggie, Sunny, and Jill
came over. We holed up in my room. The
party is tonight and we had to decide
whether to go to it.

    "Of course we're going to go," said
Sunny stubbornly.

    "We have to," I added, although I
didn't feel very certain about this.

    "Well, we really _want_ to," Maggie said.

"But let's be realistic. Do we actually think our parents are going to let us go?"

Nobody said anything for a moment.

"What would we tell them?" I finally asked. "I mean, where would we say we're going? To a secret party three miles from here given by a bunch of older kids?"

"Well..." said Sunny.

Jill finally spoke up. "It is an impossibility," she said firmly.

Sunny rolled her eyes. I shot a glance at her, but of course Jill had seen the eye-rolling for herself.

"Don't look at me like that, Sunny!" Jill exclaimed. "Come on. Get real. What are we going to tell our parents? We have to tell them we're going somewhere."

Nobody had any ideas. About getting to the party, that is. But Jill had another idea. "You guys, we can have our own party," she said. "It'll be fun. Just the four of us. Like we used to. Please?"

"Oh, man," muttered Sunny.

"What else are you going to do

tonight?" asked Jill. "Our parents aren't going to let us go to the other party."

"Well, that's true," I said.

"So come on," said Jill. "Let's go to the mall today. We can buy some stuff for our party."

"And look at clothes," added Sunny, brightening.

"And window-shop," I said.

Jill looked from Maggie to me to Sunny. Expectantly. Like a dog who's just heard his master say a whole bunch of words and is positive that one of them was "walk."

"All right," said Sunny. "Mall. Then sleepover."

Saturday afternoon 10/4

We have been to the mall. In a little while it will be time to leave for Jill's sleepover.

We had fun this afternoon. We really did. I think we're going to have fun tonight, too. I hope so. I don't like this feeling of everything changing. I feel so torn. Sometimes I'm like Jill and I just want everything to stay the way it's been. I want us to be young and safe. But sometimes I'm like Sunny, wanting to surge forward and get on with things. Impatient for whatever is coming. Not even caring what it is. Just wanting to experience it, taste it, live it.

Jill showed up at the mall with a list of things she said we needed to buy for the sleepover. It included popcorn, sodas, and fortune-telling cards.

Sunny glanced at the list. "Okay, we'll get all this stuff last. Let's look around first. How about the jewelry store?"

"Um, okay," Jill replied reluctantly. She folded the list slowly and slid it back into the pocket of her jeans.

In the jewelry store, Sunny ran to a case of pierced earrings. "Maybe I'll get another couple of holes in one of my ears," she said.

"Another couple of holes?" I replied.

"Sure. They can do that here. See that stool? That's where you sit for ear-piercing ... or navel-piercing."

"Navel-piercing!" I exclaimed.

"Ew," said Jill.

"You are not getting your navel pierced," I said. "Or getting extra holes. You have enough holes already. Why don't you just buy some more earrings? Here. Look at these. These are cute."

"I guess," agreed Sunny. "But I want something a little ... I don't know ... wilder. Like these."

"Those?" I said. "They're just plain gold hoops."

"They are eyebrow rings," said Sunny.

"Ew," Jill said again.

"Maybe we've looked long enough in here," said Maggie. "Let's go to the pet store. I need some supplies."

"Goody, we can look at the kittens!" exclaimed Jill.

Sunny rolled her eyes.

I pulled her aside. "Sunny," I

whispered, "quit doing that, okay? _Please_?
Jill is going to see you. Let's just have a
nice afternoon."

Sunny's response was to roll her eyes
again. "Tsk."

"What is _wrong_?" I said, exasperated.
And then I caught myself. "Is it your
mother?" I whispered.

Sunny turned away from me. "We can
talk about it later."

"Okay," I said, putting my arm
around her shoulder.

We hurried out of the jewelry store
and caught up with Maggie and Jill,
who were heading into World of Pets.

"What supplies do you need?" I
asked Maggie.

"Let me see. Fish food, a water bottle
for Cosmo's cage, a new bell toy for
Curtis, and — you won't believe this —
tartar-control dry food and a feline
toothbrush for Herman."

I started to giggle. "What?" I
said.

Maggie was laughing too. "I took

Herman to the vet yesterday after school and he's developing gingivitis. So I am supposed to brush his teeth every other day."

"You can really buy toothbrushes for cats?" I asked.

"Apparently."

"Wow. What does your mom think of all this?"

"Oh, who knows. All she cares about is where her next pair of shoes is coming from. I think she and her friends must be having some sort of contest to see who can buy the most expensive clothes. And Dad thinks I'm crazy, of course. He says when he was my age he had already started making films. Amateur ones, but still. He can't believe I want to be a vet. Oh, look. Feline toothbrushes."

Sure enough. There they were. Maggie tossed one into her basket, which already held the fish food, water bottle, and bell toy. Then she added a couple of dog toys and a box of catnip. Maggie has unlimited money, but you never know it except for when she's generous to the rest of us — and to her pets.

"Where are Sunny and Jill?" Maggie asked a few minutes later. "Are they together somewhere?"

"I don't know. They're not a good combination, are they?"

"Not lately."

I glanced around the store. Sunny and Jill were standing side by side, looking into a cage full of hamsters. They were pointing at something and laughing. Like old times.

Like last month.

Later Saturday afternoon 10/4
Well, I have to leave for Jill's soon, but I haven't finished writing about the mall trip. So I'll add some more here, before Carol takes Sunny and me over to Jill's.

After World of Pets we looked in a couple of clothing stores and then Jill insisted we go into this one store called The Bear Necessities. I'd never seen it before, but Jill seemed intimate with it. It was full of — guess what — teddy bears. And accessories for teddy bears and things with teddy bears on them and books about teddy bears and kits for making teddy bears. There was also a huge section of dolls and stuffed animals.

Jill was in heaven. When we left the store (with much eye-rolling on Sunny's part), she was carrying a bag containing a strip of teddy bear stickers, a pair of teddy bear barrettes, and a plastic perfume bottle shaped like a pony (with a sparkly blue mane).

"Let's eat," I said. "I'm starved."

"Cool," replied Sunny. "I mean, cool, let's eat, not cool, you're starved. Want to go to Rico's?"

"Do they have salad at Rico's?" asked Maggie.

"Do they have lemonade?" asked Jill.

We went to Starburst's, which has everything.

We sat at a booth, we ordered our food, it arrived quickly, and we were all sitting around eating and gabbing and sampling

each other's lunches when suddenly Sunny
burst into tears.

"What's the matter?" I asked her,
alarmed.

"Did they give you the wrong meal?"
asked Jill.

"Do you really think she'd cry because
they brought the wrong meal?" asked
Maggie, giving Jill an odd look.

"Besides, she's been eating it for ten
minutes," I pointed out.

"Well..." said Jill.

Maggie put her arm around Sunny.
"What is it?" she asked.

Sunny tried to smile. "Oh, it's so
stupid. I was just, like, thinking about my
mom? And I remembered the last time I
visited her in the hospital. Thursday, I
guess. And she had said she was actually
hungry, that for once she was looking
forward to her dinner, even if it was a
hospital meal. And then her food came and
she couldn't eat it after all. She just looked
at it. Then she said the smell was making
her sick, so Dad took her tray out in the

hall." Sunny paused. "And here I am stuffing my face. It is so unfair. Mom weighs like a hundred pounds. She looks like a stupid skeleton."

We all said silly, soothing things then. And I reminded myself to be extra, extra, EXTRA nice to Sunny.

I wonder if "extra nice" extends to navel rings.

I CANNOT believe it, but sometime after we had finished lunch, Sunny said to the rest of us, " I'll meet you guys at the main entrance in half an hour, okay? "

"Where are you going?" Jill asked her.

"You'll see." Sunny ran off.

Half an hour later, she met up with us like she'd promised. She was smiling smugly.

"Okay. What did you do?" I asked.

Sunny pulled her shirt up a few inches.

Glinting on her belly button was a gold ring.

"You _pierced_ your _navel_? " I hissed. I couldn't say the words out loud.

"Cool, huh? "

"What are your parents going to say?" Jill whispered. I guess she couldn't quite speak either.

"Nothing. They'll never see it. I'll just keep it covered up when they're around. Come on, let's go." Sunny turned and headed for the doors.

I wanted to yell after her, "What about bathing suits?" but I didn't. Maggie and Jill didn't say anything either. We just followed Sunny out the door, our mouths open.

Sunday night 10/5

So much has happened since that last diary entry that I hardly know how to begin writing it all down. It's going to take forever. I hope I can explain things. This is the first spare moment I've had since I left for Jill's house yesterday. That was only twenty-four hours ago. But it might as well have been two years ago.

I feel like a different person.

A very scared, nervous, confused person.

I guess I should start with yesterday when Carol drove Sunny and me to Jill's house in her red convertible. Jeff was with us. That was because he and Carol were going to go out for dinner before they went to King Hotshot to play miniature golf. I kept looking at Carol. I was surprised that she was going out to eat and then to play miniature golf. I mean, most women are sick to their stomachs all the time when they're first pregnant. Plus, they get really, really tired. But here was Carol on her way to eat Mexican food and play golf with a ten-year-old.

This was when I began to wonder if everything was all right with Carol's pregnancy. Maybe there was a problem after all. Maybe that was why Carol didn't seem so excited. I wish I could talk to Sunny about Carol, but Carol has sworn me to secrecy. Besides, Sunny has enough problems of her own.

We drove out to Jill's house with Jeff making annoying duck noises the entire way. He was sitting in the front seat wearing a Donald Duck mask. Sunny and I sat in the back with a bag of gorp between us. It was our contribution to the sleepover. We also had our sleeping bags and overnight bags.

"Remember when we would go to slumber parties and our overnight bags held candy and stuffed animals?" Sunny asked me.

"Yeah," I said fondly.

"This time I packed clothes and makeup. Like I was going on a business trip. You know what Lorna Tobias took to her last slumber party?"

"What?" I asked.

"A cell phone."

"Quack, quack," said Jeff.

"I feel so old," I said.

"Me too," said Sunny.

"Here we are," called Carol.

"Thanks!" said Sunny and I as we scrambled out of the car.

"We'll call you tomorrow!" I added.

"Okay. 'Bye!" called Carol.

"Quack, quack," said Jeff again.

"He is so weird," Sunny said as we walked to the Hendersons' door.

Jill flung the door open before I could ring the bell. "Hi, you guys!" she cried. "Come on in. Maggie just called. She'll be here in about twenty minutes. Something to do with their chauffeur. That'll be perfect timing. I just ordered the pizzas. They should get here just about when Maggie does. Too bad the pizza guy couldn't pick her up on his way." Jill seemed to think this was very funny.

Sunny smiled politely. I nudged her. The second Jill turned her back for a moment, I elbowed Sunny. "Be. Nice." I mouthed this to her. She got the point.

The thing is, Sunny and Jill used to be close friends. Just like Sunny and Maggie, and Sunny and me. This is just one of the many things that are changing.

It nearly made me cry.

Twenty minutes later, just as Jill had predicted, the pizza guy and Maggie arrived at the same time. The pizza guy arrived in a white van with PAPA'S PIZZA painted on the side, only you could see where it had once said ARACE: FOR ALL YOUR SEASONAL FURNISHINGS AND DECORATIONS.

Maggie arrived in a sleek black limo.

"Whoa," said the pizza guy.

Maggie ignored him. She breezed into the house, scowling. I knew what was wrong.

"I _hate_ that!" Maggie cried. She meant arriving in the limo. She thinks it's pretentious. She's also afraid that people will only like her because of her money and her father's connections. "At least Lena was driving, and she was on her way home so she was just wearing jeans and a sweater. The worst is when they wear the suit with the cap."

Out on the front porch I could hear the pizza guy ask Jill, "Is she famous or something?"

"No," said Jill. "But her father is a producer. He knows John Travolta. And Demi Moore. Gwyneth Paltrow too."

"No kidding?" said the guy.

"Yes, she is kidding!" Maggie yelled, even though that was the truth. "I'm nobody!"

"Oh, Maggie," I said.

"I cannot wait until I'm a vet. I'll drive around in an old station wagon, rescuing wounded animals and finding homes for them. And I'll live in a normal house and no one will think twice about me. Except my patients."

"You could change your name to Doctor Dolittle," said Sunny.

"Very funny," said Maggie, but she was smiling.

Jill's mom wouldn't let us take the pizza upstairs to eat in Jill's room, but she did leave the kitchen so we could eat there in privacy. As soon as the dishes were cleared away, though, Jill said, "_Now_ let's go upstairs. I've got a big surprise there for you."

The big surprise was that Jill had wheeled the TV and the VCR from her mom's room into her room. Plus, her room was all decorated.

"What's this?" asked Sunny.

"I decorated. For us," Jill said.

"Oh. . . . Very, um, festive," I told her.

Jill's decorations consisted of pink and white streamers, a pink and white string of letters that spelled out BACK TO SCHOOL!, and bunches of pink and white balloons.

"It looks like a birthday cake," added Sunny. This time I couldn't tell if she was being mean or trying to be nice.

Jill couldn't tell either. "Well...thanks," she said finally. "Okay, are we ready to party?"

Late Sunday night 10/5

I should definitely be asleep now, considering what is going to happen tomorrow. I mean, what is probably going to happen. I'm sure Ms. Krueger is going to want to see Sunny and me. And Ducky. In her office. Which is why I can't sleep. Anyway, I need to catch up with myself. I'm still writing about last night — and there's been a lifetime between then and now.

Somehow, I don't think that the person who coined the phrase "Are we ready to party?" meant with pink and white balloons, popcorn, and a selection of Disney videos for the VCR. I'm pretty sure he or she had something more sophisticated in mind.

But when Jill asked that question last night, I called out cheerfully, "Yeah! Par-TY!"

Sunny looked at me like I was crazy. Then she yawned. "What are we going to do all night?" she whined.

"What are we going to do?" Jill repeated. "Well, we can watch any of these Disney movies. Look. I have *Pocahontas* and *The Little Mermaid* and" (she saw our interest waning) "and some older ones that aren't cartoons. *Mary Poppins* and *Pollyanna*."

"Oh, *Pollyanna*," said Maggie. "I haven't seen that since I was little."

"Great! We'll watch it now," said Jill.

"Oh, no, no. That's okay. I didn't mean that. I meant . . . I just meant . . . let's watch something older."

Jill frowned. She looked through some other videos. "Well," she said at last, "I have *Babe*."

"You know what?" said Sunny. "I'm not in the mood for a movie."

This was too bad. Sunny should not have opened her mouth. Guess why. Because Jill had about a thousand other plans for the evening, each of them way worse than watching one of the movies.

First she forced a game of charades on us. When that excitement died down, she said, "Okay, now let's goof—call the neighbors. Oh, wait. We can't do that yet. We'll have to wait until Mom and Liz leave."

Sunny's head snapped up. "Your mom and sister are leaving?" she asked. "When? Soon?"

Jill looked at her watch. "Yup. In about fifteen minutes."

"Really." Sunny looked like a scientist with an important new piece of information. "Hmmm..."

Jill didn't seem to notice Sunny. "Okay! Let's play Cootie!"

This time even Maggie couldn't help herself. "Cootie? Get real! We're not going to play Cootie," she exclaimed.

"Oh, please," added Sunny. (She said it in exasperation.)

Jill bit her lip. "Um, okay. Then how about... makeovers?"

Sunny snorted.

That was too much for Jill. "All right. What do _you_ want to do, Sunny? You go ahead and run the party."

Sunny didn't say anything. For a moment I thought she was gathering her courage to apologize to Jill. But she just kept scowling, and finally a strange expression came over Jill's face. "You don't want to be here, do you, Sunny?" she said. "You didn't really want to have a sleepover, did you? You think they're babyish. You just went along with the idea because you can't go to the other party. Isn't that right?"

"Well..." Sunny said.

"I knew it!" exclaimed Jill. "I knew it!" She turned angrily to Maggie and me. "How about you guys? Did you guys want to have a sleepover? _Did_ you?"

"Well, sleepovers used to be fun," Maggie replied.

I thought that was a very diplomatic answer, but it made Jill burst into tears.

"Jill," I said. "Come on."

I started to put my arm around her, but she jerked away. "Leave me alone. Just —"

"Ji—ill!" I heard Mrs. Henderson call from downstairs.

Jill opened her door. "What?"

"Your sister and I are leaving now. We'll be back around midnight. You girls have fun. If you need anything, the Bergens are home. Mr. Bergen said they'll be up late tonight."

"Okay!" Jill called. "'Bye!"

"'Bye, honey."

A moment later I heard the front door close. Then I heard a car start and pull out of the driveway.

I was about to say something to Jill, to try and make up with her, when Sunny said, looking thoroughly sneaky, "Well, now's our chance."

"To do what?" I asked.

"To go to the other party. The *real* party," she couldn't help adding. When no one said anything she went on, "We could walk over there. We couldn't have from our neighborhood. But here at Jill's house we're halfway there."

"It's still a really long walk," said Maggie. She looked excited, though.

"But we can do it. Easy," Sunny hurried on.

"Well . . . I guess we could." Guess who said that. Me. I was surprised to hear those words come from my mouth.

But not as surprised as Jill was. "Dawn!" she said with a gasp.

I barely heard her. I looked at Maggie and Sunny. "Should we?"

"Of course!" exclaimed Sunny.

"Wait a sec," said Maggie. "Just let me think. Okay. The party begins at ten. And Jill's mom will be back at midnight. We can get to the party in half an hour." She checked her watch. "And it's only nine now. We could stay at the party for an hour and easily be back before Mrs. Henderson gets back."

"Cool," said Sunny.

"Great," I said.

"No way," said Jill.

We all looked at her. "But Jill," said Maggie.

"No way," Jill said again. "What if we get caught? What if the Bergens call to check on us and no one answers the phone?"

"Are the Bergens your baby-sitters?" asked Sunny.

"No!" cried Jill.

"Well, _we_ want to go to the party," said Maggie.

Jill crossed her arms. "Okay. If you guys want to go, then go."

"Okay, we will," I said.

And we did.

Monday 10/6

Well, it is now 5:30 Monday morning. I got about four hours of sleep last night. I _tried_ to sleep. I just couldn't. I lay in bed and my thoughts whirled around. I actually tried counting sheep. When I reached 5,000 I gave up. What a stupid idea.

My alarm clock was set for 6:30, but I already turned it off. At about 5:20 my eyes flew open. I knew they wouldn't close

again. Not without help. Glue or something.
So finally I turned on my light.

We didn't leave Jill's house that very
second. First Sunny and Maggie and I all
had to go to the bathroom and then we had
to get a few things together. Plus, I tried
to be nice to Jill.
"Are you _sure_ you don't want to come
with us?" I said to her. "It'll be fun. An
adventure. You like adventures. Please?"
Jill relaxed a little. She smiled at me.
But she shook her head. "No. I can't go.
Maybe I do like adventures. But not this
kind."
"Okay."
"Do you _promise_ you guys will be
back before midnight?"
"Promise," I said.
"Cross your heart?"
I crossed my heart.
When Maggie and Sunny and I left
awhile later, we were each carrying a purse,
and our purses were fatter than usual. Two
of us were carrying flashlights in case we

had to walk down any road that didn't have streetlights. And Maggie's sandals were in her purse. She wanted to wear them at the party but said they'd give her blisters if she hiked around in them.

The walk to the party seemed to take forever, and some of the streets were pretty dark. We got out our flashlights four times. Sunny was the only one of us who knew where she was going, and I was glad she did.

"How do you know your way around out here?" Maggie asked her.

"From taking bike rides with my parents. Before, you know, before Mom got sick."

"Oh," said Maggie and I.

"Let me see the invitation again," Sunny said then. Maggie pulled hers out of her purse and handed it to Sunny. "Thanks. Okay. We should be almost there. It should be down that road."

We were in an area on the outskirts of Palo City that I'd never been in before. The houses were huge, but their yards were huger. There were only a few houses on each road — and a lot of woods between them.

"What time is it?" I asked.

Maggie looked at her watch. "Twenty after ten."

"Perfect," said Sunny.

Suddenly I could hear voices. "Listen," I hissed.

We listened.

"Party time!" cried Sunny.

Sunny had found the house, all right. It was dark (and locked, as I found out later), but the yard was lit with lanterns and strings of lights. Two spotlights lit the pool area.

"Whose house is this?" I whispered. Mostly to stall for time. I was beginning to feel nervous.

Sunny shrugged. "Who knows? That's part of the secret, I guess. Come on."

The yard was filling with kids. Only a few were in the pool because it was chilly. Plus, the invitation hadn't said to bring a bathing suit. I noticed that the kids who were in the pool were swimming with their clothes on. Well, okay, to be more accurate, they weren't swimming. They were making out on floats.

"Do you guys see anyone you recognize?" whispered Maggie.

"Actually, I do," I replied. "Quite a few."

"Quite a few older kids too," added Sunny.

The eighth-graders were easy to tell apart from the upperclassmen. They were the ones who looked totally uncomfortable as they sipped from plastic cups or tried to light cigarettes.

"What do you suppose they're drinking?" I asked. On a table near the pool was a huge bowl filled with some kind of pale liquid. It seemed to be the only thing to drink. I didn't see any food at all.

"I don't know, but I plan to find out," replied Sunny. She started to march across the lawn toward the pool.

"Wait!" I cried.

"What?" said Sunny. "Why?"

"Just... wait. I mean, don't leave us yet. Let's stick together for a few minutes. I want to, you know, check things out."

"And don't we have to tell someone

we're here?" asked Maggie. "Who's giving the party? Shouldn't we find them and say thanks for inviting us? We should at least introduce ourselves."

"I don't know." Sunny looked doubtful. "I don't think this is that kind of party. That sounds like a cocktail party for old people. This one is more cool."

"Well, just stay with us for a few minutes," I begged Sunny. "Okay? Then you can go."

"Okay," agreed Sunny.

We stationed ourselves near a lounge chair not far from the pool and took a good look around. Music was playing loudly — but I wasn't sure where it was coming from. Someone must have set up speakers or boom boxes somewhere. Kids were clustered throughout the yard. One strange thing: I had sort of thought that the purpose of the party was for the upperclassmen to get to know us eighth-graders, at least us select few eighth-graders. But I didn't see much mingling going on. I saw lots of little groups of older kids, and lots of little groups of eighth—graders, but hardly any mixed groups.

And now, as the sun rises slowly in the east, I hear Carol's clock radio going off, so I'll have to stop here for awhile. It's time to get ready for school.

School. Dum—de—dum—dum.

Thank goodness I'll have my journal to turn to today.

Monday 10/6, in study hall

Maggie and Sunny and I were standing at the party in a tight knot just trying to get the feel of things. I noticed that the groups of older kids were a little more animated than us eighth—graders. They were laughing and talking loudly. One guy kept throwing kids in the pool. And they were all drinking whatever was in that bowl on the table. A lot of them were smoking, too. They seemed to have an endless supply of cigarettes. The cigarettes kept appearing out of people's sleeves, pockets, shirt cuffs, and purses.

"Okay," said Sunny after a few minutes of watching things. "Now I'm going to go. I want to talk to people."

"We're people," I said, but Sunny didn't hear me.

"I'm coming with you," Maggie said.

"So am I." I could feel those butterflies in my stomach.

Sunny made a beeline for the table with the punch. Maggie and I were at her heels. Sunny had just reached for a cup when a very cute guy (I think he's a junior) stuck a pack of cigarettes under her nose. It was all fixed so that two cigarettes were sticking out, one a little further than the other. Very cool. Sunny was supposed to take the one that was sticking out the furthest. I have seen this in movies many times.

But this was not a movie, so things didn't go quite as planned. Sunny wanted to be cool. And she reached for the cigarette — but with just the slightest hesitation.

"Is something wrong?" asked the guy.

Sunny turned on an absolutely charming

smile. But I knew she didn't want the cigarette. I also knew why.

"Oh," I said to the guy. "She doesn't smoke. Her mother's dying of lung cancer. Thanks anyway."

"Whatever," the guy said, and left.

I watched Sunny. I have never seen so many emotions on a person's face at once. She was aghast at my rudeness. And she was in shock. Neither one of us has ever actually said that her mother is dying. But I could also see that she was trying not to laugh.

So was Maggie. "I can't believe you just said that!" she exclaimed.

"Me nei —" I started to say. But at that moment two girls walked over to us, each carrying several cups of punch. They handed one to me, one to Maggie, one to Sunny.

"Here you go. Try this," one said. Then they walked away.

I looked down at the cup in my hand. I sniffed at it. I could smell something vaguely fruity. Also something strong.

"Well, down the hatch!" said Sunny.

And she chugged her entire cup, her head tossed back.

Maggie took a sip of hers.

"Interesting," she said slowly.

I took a sip of mine. I spit it out.

"Oh, ew! That is disgusting! Sunny, how did you drink yours? It tastes like strawberries and insect repellent." I wouldn't have been surprised if my throat had caught on fire. How _had_ Sunny drunk hers?

In all honesty, Sunny's eyes looked sort of watery. But that was it. Her head wasn't spinning around or anything. In fact, in a vaguely hoarse voice she said, "I think I'll go get a little more. See you guys. Ciao."

That was the last I saw of Sunny for quite awhile.

I looked at Maggie. "What do you think this stuff is?" I asked her.

Maggie considered. "Strawberry wine?" she suggested.

I shrugged.

Maggie set her cup down. I set mine down too. It was a good thing we'd eaten at Jill's house.

"Blech," I said. We left the mostly

full cups and wandered away from the pool. Suddenly Maggie gripped my arm. "Hey! Is that Justin Randall?" she whispered loudly.

I peered at the guy she was pointing to. "I don't think so," I said.

"Oh." Maggie sounded disappointed.

We stood around then for awhile. A long while. Until . . .

"Dawn? Maggie?" I heard someone say. It wasn't Sunny. I turned around. Standing behind us was an eighth-grade girl I sort of recognized. The new girl. The one who might be named Amelia. Or Amalia.

"Hi," I said. "Um . . ."

"It's Amalia?" she said. "Amalia Vargas? I'm in your study hall?"

"Oh, sure," I replied. "Hi. I'm . . . well, I guess you know us."

"Kind of." Amalia looked as nervous as I felt. "So you got one of the invitations too." She looked around at the party. "This is kind of weird, isn't it?"

I nodded. "Did you come by yourself?"

"Yeah. I was supposed to meet — "

Amalia stopped talking. She was stopped by someone who grabbed her arm and then burst out laughing. Very, very loudly.

"What — " Amalia started to say.

"Sunny!" I cried.

"Oh, Dawn. How nice to see you!" Sunny exclaimed. She wobbled slightly. "Isn't this fun?"

Oh, man, I thought. "Sunny — "

"Well, I need another little drink," said Sunny.

"No, you don't," said Maggie.

Sunny looked directly into Maggie's eyes. In a slow, careful voice she said, "Yes, I do. You see, I am very, very firsty. Thirsty."

Sunny turned and walked away, listing to the right.

I looked at Maggie and Amalia. Suddenly Amalia grinned. "She's sloshed!" she cried. "I'm sorry, but it's a little funny."

Maggie was smiling too. "She's not sloshed, she's shloshed."

"She'sh slossed," said Amalia.

"Shlossed," I said.

"See? We can talk like that without drinks," said Amalia.

I decided I liked Amalia.

Maggie and Amalia and I hung out for half an hour or so, goofing on people, gossiping, turning down drinks and cigarettes.

Finally, just when I realized we better pay attention to the time, I heard a pathetic voice say, "Dawn? It'sh me, Shunshine. Do you know where the barfroom lives? I mean, where the bathroom is? I need it des — disp — badly."

"Sunny! How much have you had to drink?" I demanded.

"Oh, a fair amount. That nishe boy keepsh refilling the bowl. But you know what? I feel a little, oh . . ."

That was when I noticed the awful shade of green Sunny's face had become. Green and pale at the same time.

"Oh! Ew! You're not going to barf, are you?" shrieked Amalia.

She shrieked it loudly enough so that a bunch of older girls all turned around and looked at us. With horror, I realized they were Mandy Richards and her friends.

"Barf fest!" called Mandy gleefully. "We got one!" I realized that Mandy had been hoping us eighth-graders would drink enough to get sick.

I don't think Sunny heard her. "Dawn, there ishn't mush time. Where ish the bathroom? Thish ish ekshtremely improtent."

"I — the house looks locked, Sunny."

"Oh...oh, no." Sunny put her hand to her mouth.

Amalia stepped back.

"Get her to those bushes!" cried Maggie.

I yanked Sunny over to some bushes at the side of the house. Just in time. Sunny let loose, spewing all over the bushes and her shoes. I patted her back. After a minute or two, I peered out from the bushes.

Mandy and her friends were standing nearby, smiling. Honestly, Mandy looked sort of evil. Amalia and Maggie hung back, humiliated.

"It must be her first time," I heard Mandy say. "Which figures. She's here with *Puppy Pal.*" This was followed by laughter.

I ducked back behind the bushes.

"Sunny?" I said softly.

After a pause, she replied, "Yeah?"

"Are you okay?"

"No! I just barfed all over everything. I have never barfed so much in my entire life... Wait... I'm not done yet."

After some more choking and puking, Sunny said weakly, "Okay." She stepped out of the bushes on wobbly legs, like a colt trying to stand for the first time. "Oh, my God," she said.

"What?" I replied.

"Everything is all foozy and wuzzy. I mean, fuzzy and woozy. Spinning around."

The party was beginning to seem like a very bad idea to me. I looked at my watch. We would have to leave soon. I could not believe that we still had to walk all the way back to Jill's. And with Sunny as sick as she was, it was going to take longer than it had taken to walk to the party. Which was longer than we had figured in the first place.

One big bad idea.

How was I to know it would get worse?

Well, school is over. I made it. I survived. Somehow. But the trouble isn't over. We're going to have an assembly tomorrow, which is bad enough. Worse, though, just like I thought, Ms. Krueger wants to see Sunny and Ducky and me in her office before the assembly. Now that's where trouble could lie.

But back to Saturday night, so I can explain who Ducky and Ms. Krueger are, and catch up to today.

Sunny lay down on the front stoop of the house. She said she couldn't even think about walking back to Jill's until she had recovered. I tried to get her to at least sit in a lawn chair, but she said that was too much effort. She was like a limp noodle, and she needed to lie down.

While Maggie and I waited for Sunny,

we edged away from Mandy and her friends.
Amalia stuck with us.

"Does the music seem louder to you
guys?" Amalia asked. She had to shout to
be heard.

"Yes!" I screeched back. "Definitely!"

The volume had been cranked up to an
eardrum—shattering level. The bass was so
loud that the earth seemed to be pulsing
beneath my feet. More kids had arrived at
the party. They brought beer. The louder the
music got, the louder the kids got. And the
air around us was a haze of smoke. It
stung my throat and eyes.

"Hey! Hey, there's Justin Randall!"
Maggie suddenly shrieked. "This time I
really do see him!"

"Someone else sees him too," I
remarked. "Mandy. Look."

Not far from us, Mandy eyed Justin,
turned, whispered something to one of her
friends, then gazed at Justin again.

It was at this moment, this precise
moment (I'll never forget it), that I
heard the cry of, "Everybody in the pool!"

That was it. It was like unexpected

lightning on a summer night. The sky is clear, no storm clouds, then, without warning, lightning flashes — and hits a tree.

Same thing at the party. Everyone was just standing around, then someone yelled, "Everybody in the pool!" and in the very next second grabbed a nearby girl and threw her in the pool. Then he reached for another person and another.

The first girl came up sputtering. "Hey! My watch!" she yelled.

No one paid attention to her.

The boy who had thrown her in the pool was still grabbing other kids and flinging them in the pool. They didn't look any more pleased about it than the girl had.

Three of them were scrambling out while more kids were being thrown in, and the next thing I knew, a pair of hands had grabbed me and I felt myself being lifted in the air.

"Hey!" I cried.

Next to me, someone had grabbed Maggie. And in the next moment we were flying through the air.

I nearly landed on Maggie but

managed to avoid her. I didn't know whether to cry or laugh. I chose laughter. Giggling, I dog-paddled to the side of the pool and hoisted myself out. Maggie followed me to the edge but remained in the chilly water, only her head sticking out.

I held out my hand to her. "Come on," I said. Maggie shook her head. "No? What's wrong?"

Before Maggie could answer, I felt myself being grabbed again. I did NOT want to be tossed into that pool for a second time, so I clutched at someone who was standing next to me. I only meant to regain my balance ... not push Mandy Richards in the pool.

But that's what happened.

When Mandy hoisted herself out of the pool, she just glared at me. I had thought earlier that she looked sort of evil. Now I saw that she looked thoroughly evil.

I shuddered.

Then I turned back to Maggie. "Come on," I said again. (This time my voice was shaking.)

"I can't," she hissed. "I'm only wearing a T-shirt. And it's really thin. You can see right through it. You can see everything. And I mean everything. I'm not wearing a bra." (Maggie should _always_ wear a bra.)

"Maggie, you can't stay in there forever." Although frankly I thought she looked safer in there, out of Mandy's reach.

"Yes, I can," said Maggie, but she only lasted for about three minutes. Then she climbed out of the pool, stood up — and found herself face-to-face with Justin Randall.

I watched the expressions that crossed Justin's face. The one I expected (and that Maggie expected), the leer that would have humiliated her, never showed up. What I saw first was simple surprise as Maggie suddenly stood up before him, then more surprise when he saw her T-shirt, and then . . . admiration.

His eyes widened. "Whoa," he said.

I was standing next to Maggie in my big old jean jacket (not that there would have been much to see even without it), and I watched Justin. I suppose I should have stepped aside (just like I should have hung up the phone when Carol's doctor called), but I couldn't. Which is why I saw Mandy standing next to us in her wet dress, which was now as tantalizingly clingy as Maggie's T-shirt. But Justin never noticed her. He couldn't drag his eyes away from Maggie. (Well, from her ample chest.) They were glued to her.

I smiled to myself. And I almost shot a triumphant smirk at Mandy. But then I realized that she was looking at _me._ I don't think she had even noticed Maggie. Her look chilled me. Why couldn't I have grabbed at someone else ... at anyone else but Mandy? She will never forget what I did to her.

I turned away.

Someone jostled Justin then, and the moment ended. I took Maggie by the arm. "We better go," I said. "It's going to take forever to walk back with Sunny in her ... condition."

Maggie and I, dripping and chilly,

found Sunny lolling on the porch. "Okay, time to go!" I said cheerfully.

"Oh, no, I couldn't possibly," Sunny replied, moaning.

"Well, you have to. Jill's mother is going to be home at midnight. We don't want her to catch us. And we certainly don't want her to see you like this."

"But I feel so horrible."

"Sunny, what do you want to do, then?" asked Maggie, frustrated. "Call Mrs. Henderson and ask her to come pick us up?"

While Sunny and Maggie argued (Sunny weakly, and Maggie urgently), I looked around. Something seemed wrong. It took me about half a second to figure out what. The party was ending — abruptly. The upperclassmen were all hustling out of the yard. The punch table had been abandoned. And the only things in the pool were the things that had been thrown in after the people were thrown in. Lawn furniture, a bicycle, and a number of unidentifiable objects that were sinking to the bottom. The yard was empty except for most of us eighth-graders and a whole lot of trash. Cups and papers were everywhere, trampled into the yard and gardens.

"Hey, you guys," I said cautiously. And quietly. The music had ended too. "Um, I think the party's over."

"You're not kidding," muttered Maggie. "Look."

I didn't have to look. I could _hear_. Sirens and slamming doors as two squad cars pulled into the driveway and several officers stepped out. "The police!" I shrieked.

Maggie clapped her hand over my mouth. "We have to get out of here. Now! Let's go, Sunny."

Maggie took off into the woods behind the house. Our choice was to follow her or to be caught. Sunny and I followed. We sprinted across the lawn. The moment we reached the woods, Sunny slowed down, though. "I _truly_ cannot go as fast as you guys are going," she said. She was speaking awfully loudly, though. She now looked sort of hearty and cheerful, even if she was a little weak.

"Sunny, be quiet!" I hissed.

Sunny grinned. "Let me see, now. Where did that road go?" she asked. She had not lowered her voice one bit. "All right, everybody. This way! Let's go!"

Monday night 10/6

It is so weird to think that I had this incredible adventure over the weekend, and Carol has no idea. No idea. Not a clue. All she knows is that I went to a sleepover at Jill's.

I don't like that. I mean, I don't want to be in trouble with Carol. On the other hand, it kind of bothers me that I got away with something so major. It doesn't seem right. I feel uncomfortable.

I'm not explaining myself very well.

Maggie and Sunny and I crashed through the underbrush, heading in what Sunny swore was the direction of the road the house was on. We needed to find that road. But believe me, we did not want to wind up too close to the house. I was sure the police were there looking for people.

After stumbling around for fifteen minutes or so (Sunny complaining at the top of her lungs every inch of the way), I thought I could see a streetlight ahead. We headed for the light and emerged on a narrow street. We were still out in the middle of nowhere, but luckily we were near an intersection — one tiny dark road crossing another. A street sign was lit by the lamp. I read the two names aloud.

"I don't recognize either of them," said Maggie nervously.

"I do," said Sunny. "Let me see! Which direction should we take?! Okay, that road is Verdes —"

"That'll run into Mango, won't it?" I asked.

"Oh, please. Do _not_ mention food!" shouted Sunny.

"Sorry," I said. "But I still don't know whether to turn left or right."

"I do," said a voice that did not belong to Sunny or Maggie (or me). I whirled around.

Amalia was emerging from the woods.

"But it doesn't matter," Amalia continued, "because I am dead meat."

"You are?" I asked.

"Absolutely. I left my house three hours ago, saying that I had a baby-sitting job and I'd be home by 11:30. It's after midnight now."

"It _is_?" shrieked Maggie. "I had no idea. I guess my watch stopped when I was thrown in the pool."

"Well, then we must be dead meat too!" cried Sunny.

"Hey! Headlights!" exclaimed Amalia. "Get out of the road! It might be the police. Get back in the woods."

But Sunny stumbled, and we all fell over her. We were still recovering from our pileup when the car slowed down and pulled over and a familiar-looking guy leaned out and said, "Are you all right?" When we didn't answer right away, he said, "Hello? Excuse me? Can I help you?"

I was trying to remember where I'd seen this guy before. I was still struggling when Amalia said timidly, "Oh...hi.

You're, um, you're in my study hall. I mean, in ours." Amalia pointed to me. "I think."

Then I remembered. He was the nice guy. The one everyone seemed to like.

The guy leaned further out of the car. "Oh, yeah," he said. "That's right. Anyway, I saw you at the party. Can I give you all a ride? This isn't – "

He was interrupted by a shriek from Sunny, and Amalia turned to her in alarm. "You're not going to barf again, are you?" she asked.

"No!" cried Sunny. "But I just realized that my wallet's gone."

"Are you sure?" I asked.

"Yes. It's probably back at the party."

"Oh, great," I said. "And now the police are at the party. If they find your wallet, they'll know we were there too. Or at least that you were. It's full of identification."

"Hello?" said the boy again.

"We are in so much trouble," Maggie said slowly.

"Excuse me? Hello?" said the guy.

" How far did we come from the party? " Sunny asked him.

"About . . . let me see . . . about a quarter of a mile."

" A <u>quarter</u> of a mile? You're kidding. I feel like we walked two miles. At least, " said Amalia.

" Can you drive us back there? " Sunny asked the guy.

"To the party? No way. The yard is crawling with cops. They're everywhere. They're taking a bunch of kids down to the station."

Sunny sank down by the side of the road. I think she meant to sit on a rock, but she missed it and sat on the muddy ground instead.

" Well, this is it, " said Sunny. " My life is over. "

Later Monday night 10/6

I have turned into an insomniac. I've been trying to fall asleep for the last hour and a half, and nothing is happening. Finally

I decided to get up and continue the story in my journal. At the moment, I wish it were a made-up story. Unfortunately, it's true.

"Hey," said the guy. "I very much doubt that your life is over. Come on. Get in the car. I'll drive you wherever you need to go. Okay? I mean, it's a start." He pointed to his beat-up old car. "Come on. Climb in. I might not get you guys wherever you need to go on time, but it'll be better than stumbling around in the woods in the middle of the night, won't it?" He reached across the seat and opened the passenger door.

Maggie, Sunny, Amalia, and I all did the same thing at once. In unison we started for the car. Then we hesitated. We nearly had another pileup. I mean, who was this guy we were about to trust with our lives? A familiar face from study hall. That was all.

The guy must have read my mind. "Oh. Sorry. You don't even know my name, do

you? Well, it's Christopher McCrae. Guess
what everyone calls me, though?"

"Um, Chris?" I guessed.

He shook his head. "Nope. Ducky. From
that Molly Ringwald movie, _Pretty in Pink_. I
saw it when I was a kid, and everyone in
my family thought I was a young Ducky,
so they started calling me that, and the
name just stuck. Anyway, I'm sixteen years
old, I'm in tenth grade at Vista, and I
enjoy speed-reading, gourmet cooking, and
fly-fishing."

I giggled. Ducky seemed okay. He
certainly seemed more okay than wandering
around in the woods or getting arrested.
Maggie, Sunny, and Amalia must have
thought so too, because the next thing I
knew, the four of us had piled into his car.

"Evening, ladies," said Ducky. He put
a baseball cap on his head. "I am Pierre
and I will be your chauffeur for the
evening. Where to?"

"Well, three of us are going —" I
started to say and then realized that _we_
hadn't introduced ourselves to Ducky yet.

"Oh, wait! Um, Ducky, I'm Dawn Schafer —"

"And I'm Amalia Vargas," Amalia interrupted me. "We're the ones who are in your study hall."

"And that's Maggie Blume," I said, pointing. "And that's Sunny Winslow, the one who is currently wallet-free."

"And ill," Sunny croaked.

I turned to Sunny in alarm. She was sitting in the backseat between Maggie and me.

"*Now* are you going to barf again?" Amalia asked her.

"Um, maybe. The car is making me —"

Ducky stopped the car with a little screech of the brakes. "Why don't you sit up front? Next to the window. I mean, since I just had the car cleaned and all."

Sunny, Amalia, and I slid out of the car and traded places so that Sunny could sit next to Ducky. He helpfully rolled her window all the way down for her.

When we were settled, Ducky took off again.

"So *where* are we going?" he asked.

"Well, Sunny and Maggie and I are all going to the same place," I said. I told him how to get to Jill's house.

"And I'm going to Royal Lane," added Amalia. "Off of Longwood."

"When do you have to be home?" I asked Ducky.

"No particular time. It doesn't matter. My brother's out late tonight."

"Your brother? What about your parents?" Maggie asked him, and I nudged her. What if his parents were dead or something?

"Oh, my parents trust me," said Ducky. (He sailed over a bump in the road and I saw Sunny edge closer to the window.) "Anyway, there isn't much they can do from Accra."

"Accra?" repeated Maggie.

"Yeah, in Africa. Ghana. They're there for a year. They're professors. So it's just my brother and me."

"How old's your brother?" asked Amalia.

"Twenty. He's a junior at Palo Tech. But he's living at home this year. That way my parents didn't have to make any arrangements for me while they're gone. It's kind of a weird situation, I guess, but it's working okay."

"Cool," said Maggie.

"How long have you had your car?" asked Amalia.

"I got her the day I turned sixteen," said Ducky. "She's a 1972 Buick, so she's older than I am. I paid $450 for her. She was worth every penny."

"She's ... beautiful," I said, as I nearly lost my hand down an enormous hole in the seat. "Very retro."

I was so fascinated by Ducky and his car that I had almost forgotten about the trouble we were in. Then Ducky said, "Okay, Amalia, here's Royal Lane. Where's your house?"

Amalia closed her eyes briefly. "The third one on the left." She opened her eyes and leaned forward to peer ahead. "It's dark," she said. "I don't know what that means, whether it's good or bad."

Ducky slowed down, then stopped in front of the house. "Do you want me to wait?" he asked Amalia.

"No. You better go," she said, whispering now. "I'll see you all in school on Monday." She scrambled out of the car.

Ducky turned the car around and we started off again, this time in a quieter mood.

"So how come you're all going to the same address?" Ducky asked, glancing in the rearview mirror.

Maggie told him about Jill and the sleepover.

"You think her mother and sister are home by now?" he said.

"Who has a working watch?" asked Sunny sullenly.

"I do," said Ducky. "It's 12:40."

"I'm positive they're home," replied Sunny.

After a pause Ducky said, "If you want, I could come get you guys tomorrow morning. I could take you back to the house where the party was, and we could look for your wallet, Sunny."

"But won't someone see us?" she asked.

"Um, no. No one's home. I mean, they're gone for the weekend."

I had the unpleasant feeling that Ducky

was leaving something out, but Sunny brightened. "Would you really do that?" she asked.

"Sure," replied Ducky, brightening himself. "I'd be happy to. I'll come get you at eleven tomorrow, okay?"

"Cool!" she cried.

"Well, here we are," Ducky said a few moments later as he stopped in front of the Hendersons'.

I peered out the window. Like Maggie's house, Jill's was dark. Not a single light on.

"Maybe they're not back," I suggested.

"No, they're back," said Maggie. "If they were still out, the porch light would be on, at least."

We slithered out of Ducky's car and waved at him as he pulled away and drove down the street. Then we headed for the front door.

Early Tuesday morning 10/7
An almost sleepless night. If things don't get straightened out soon I'll have

bags under my eyes big enough to carry stuff in. It's 4:45 AM. I've been awake since 4:10. I can write for almost two hours before anyone gets up around here.

"Well, now what should we do?"

Sunny and Maggie and I were standing halfway up the Hendersons' lawn, gazing at the dark house.

"Which window is Jill's?" asked Sunny loudly.

"That one," I said, pointing to the second story. "And the one next to it. Hey, I think a little light is on in her room!"

"Should we call to her?" asked Maggie. "Which one is her mother's window?" Maggie looked awfully nervous.

"Her mother's room is in the back," I said. "But don't <u>call</u> to Jill. Here." I picked up a small stone and tossed it at one of Jill's windows. It banged against the screen.

Nothing.

"Throw another," said Sunny, not quite so loudly. She looked sort of miserable again. She was lying on the front stoop, cradling her head in her arms.

Four stones later, Jill suddenly yanked up her window shade. She waved crossly at us, then disappeared.

"Oh, boy. She's still mad," said Maggie.

"_Still_ mad," repeated Sunny. "No, I think she's mad _again_. She has way more things to be mad about now." Sunny sat up. "Oh. Oh, do I ever feel sick again."

Two minutes later, Jill quietly unlocked the front door and opened it — just in time to hear Sunny retching in the bushes.

"_What_ —? _Ew_ ... What is —? Oh, _ew!_" Jill closed the door in our faces. If it hadn't been so late at night, I think she would have slammed it.

I stood there staring at the door. Finally I called, "Jill?"

The door opened a crack. "What is going on?" whispered Jill. "Where have you been? Is Sunny finished throwing up? _Why_ is she throwing up — out here? Couldn't she at least have waited until she got inside? That is so disgusting."

I looked at Maggie. I didn't know

which question to answer first. So instead I asked Jill a question. "Where is your mom?"

"She's here. She's in bed."

"Well, where does she think we are?"

Jill glanced at Sunny, who had finished puking and had sunk down on the porch steps. "She thinks you're here too. Asleep. I left a note for her that she found when she came home. It said we were tired and had gone to bed early. I had to lie to her for you."

With that, Jill opened the door the rest of the way and silently held it open for us. We slipped inside and she locked it behind us. Then without a word she tiptoed through the dark house and upstairs to her room. We followed her. She was wearing pajamas with feet in them.

"Don't you want to know what happened to us?" Maggie asked her.

"Not really." Jill turned on her light. It was the big overhead light.

"Oh. Oh, man. That is so bright," said Sunny, moaning. She crawled onto the bed and put Jill's pillow over her head.

Jill grabbed it off. "You have been

barfing!" she cried. "I don't want your face all over my pillow!"

Sunny was too miserable to argue. She pulled off her sweatshirt and put that over her head instead.

"Look, Jill, I know you're mad —" I started to say.

"Of course I'm mad!" she cried. "I hate lying, especially to my mom. I don't know why I bothered anyway. I should have told her the truth. Why did I even cover for you?"

"We appreciate it," said Sunny in a small voice from under her sweatshirt. "We really do."

That seemed to make a difference to Jill. "You do?" she said.

"Of course we do," Maggie and I said together.

"We really did try to get home on time," I added, which wasn't exactly true. "But then things got a little out of control at the party."

"Yeah, the older kids started throwing people in the pool," said Maggie. "So then we were, um, trying to dry off so that we, um, wouldn't be quite such a mess when your mom came home."

"But it was getting later and later," I went on. "And then, just when we were ready to leave, the <u>police</u> showed up."

"The police!" exclaimed Jill, managing to look both amazed and disapproving. "Whoa."

"Yeah, we don't know why," said Maggie.

"The party was too noisy," mumbled Sunny.

"Well, anyway, we didn't want to get caught, so we just ran out of the yard — it was an outdoor party," I said, "and into the woods, but we didn't know where to go, so we sort of got lost, and even when we finally came to a road, we didn't know where we were. Luckily, Ducky — Ducky McCrae, he's a sophomore — drove by then and gave us a ride over here. And that's why we're late."

"Boy," said Jill, now looking almost sympathetic.

"And I lost my wallet," said Sunny, briefly lifting up the shirt.

"What?" said Jill.

"I lost my wallet. At the party. I think. Ducky is —"

"You lost it at the _party_?" Jill interrupted her. "Oh, that's just great. That is wonderful. When the police discover it, they'll call your house and in two seconds everyone will find out where you all really were tonight, and my mom will know I lied to her."

"Jill, this is _so_ not about you," exclaimed Sunny as loudly as she could. "This is about me. How did you manage to turn the conversation around to you? Huh?"

"_How_ did I?" Jill repeated. "Because it is too about me. I'm the one you guys ditched tonight. I'm the one who had to cover for you, to tell lies for you. I'm the one —"

Maggie jumped to her feet. "Okay, okay!" she said. "You know what? Everyone is mad. Everyone is tired. It's really late. I think we should go to sleep now and talk about this in the morning when we're feeling better."

Tuesday 10/7, in study hall

Feeling better? Ha. What a joke. When we woke up on Sunday morning, we were all exhausted, even Jill, since she'd been up later than usual the night before. And even _Sunny_, despite the fact that she had PASSED OUT.

Yes, she had truly passed out. And it wasn't until I had cried (softly), "Maggie, she's passed out!" that Jill finally understood that Sunny had gotten . . .

"Drunk? She's _drunk_?" squeaked Jill. "That's why she was throwing up? Because she got drunk? And now she's passed _out_? What do you do when someone passes out?" Jill was wringing her hands.

"You just let them sleep, I guess," I said.

"No, no. It's more dangerous than that," said Maggie.

Maggie and Jill and I stared down at Sunny, who was still sprawled on the bed. We had tried calling to her and shaking her, but she wouldn't move or wake up. She seemed to be breathing all right, though. We didn't know what else to do, so we decided we would just let her sleep until the morning.

"Let's take some of her clothes off, though," said Maggie. "We'll never get her into her nightshirt, but let's take off her shoes and her jeans. She'll be more comfortable."

So that's what we did. Then we rolled her on her side and put a trash can by the bed in case of nighttime barfing. And then we had another tiff with Jill, who didn't want Sunny to sleep on her bed at all. But when we tried to move Sunny, we found that we couldn't do it easily (or quietly), so she got to sleep on the bed after all.

Then I lay awake worrying about the police. So, it turns out, did Jill and Maggie. And _then_ I had finally fallen asleep when I heard a cheerful voice say, "Time to get up, sleepyheads. I fixed you a big breakfast!"

It was Jill's sister, Liz.

I looked at my watch. Eight o'clock.

Eight o'clock? On a Sunday morning?

On <u>this</u> Sunday morning? When I had gotten, like, two and a half hours of sleep?

Before I could take this in, Mrs. Henderson bustled cheerfully into the room and snapped up the window shades.

"Rise and shine, girls!" she said. "Sunny, what are you doing sleeping in your clothes?" At that moment the tea kettle whistled shrilly from downstairs, and Mrs. Henderson hurried out of the room, leaving a cloud of perfume behind her.

"Oh, oh." Sunny was moaning loudly on the bed. "Oh, my God. The light! The noise! That smell. Oh ... ew ..."

Jill's head snapped up. "Sunny, are you going to barf?"

"I don't know. Someone pull the shades down. Make that smell go away." Luckily, the tea kettle had stopped whistling.

Jill eyed her through a curtain of tangled hair. "You're hungover, aren't you," she said. "Tsk. Disgusting."

That morning was every bit as awful as I could possibly imagine. Maggie and Jill and I weren't hungover, of course, but we were exhausted. And Jill was still mad at us, and we were still mad at her. Sunny was a different story. Her head was pounding. She said she had the worst headache she'd ever had in her life. Light bothered her. Noise bothered her. And smells made her feel sick to her stomach.

So Liz's big breakfast was torture for her. The kitchen was lit by sunshine and large fluorescent lights. Liz banged pots. The kettle whistled again. Timers buzzed and rang. And the air smelled of bacon, frying butter, coffee, and Mrs. Henderson's gardenia perfume.

I thought Sunny was going to pass out again right at the table. Somehow she managed not to, and not to barf. But she couldn't make it through breakfast. She had to tell Mrs. Henderson that she couldn't eat because she just isn't a morning person, which certainly looked believable, and then she returned to Jill's bed.

The morning passed. Sunny seemed to feel better. By eleven o'clock, she said her headache was going away. Which was good since it was time for Ducky to pick us up and take us back to the scene of the party.

"I can't go with you," said Maggie. "Unfortunately, I have to go to some charity event with Mom and Dad today. One of those huge parties with tons of celebrities at which Dad will probably hustle around making deals, and Mom will be so wrapped up in what everyone's wearing she'll forget what the charity event is _for_, which always makes me mad." Maggie sighed. "Oh, well. This party's outside. Maybe I'll find a stray cat or something."

At that moment, a car honked.

"There's Ducky," I said, and Sunny and I hurried outside before Mrs. Henderson had a chance to see that someone other than Carol was picking us up. "'Bye!" we called. "Thanks!"

"Hey!" Ducky greeted us as we clambered into his car.

In the light, his car looked different. Worse, actually. It was the oldest car I'd ever seen that wasn't an antique. Not that you'd mistake it for one of those nice antique cars. What it looked like was a junk pile.

"So how'd you guys make out last night?" Ducky asked us. He was wearing clean blue jeans and a T-shirt with a picture of Elvis on the front.

"Oh ... okay," said Sunny.

"Hungover?" Ducky asked her.

"Yeah. But now I'm better."

"I try never to get drunk," said Ducky as he left Jill's street and turned onto a main road. "In fact, I don't drink at all. Or smoke. My body is a temple. I put only the purest of things into it. Like Mountain Dew and Pez."

I smiled. "Thanks again for driving us home last night. Did you have any trouble when you got home?"

"Nope. Like I said, my brother was out. He never knew. Besides, he trusts me. So do my parents. Even long distance."

Ducky drove along, concentrating on the road, and I took a good look at him now that it was daylight. He was so earnest. And very clean-cut. He looked like someone you could really talk to. I thought of all the girls I'd seen sitting with Ducky in study hall. Did Ducky want to be our friend now? I hoped so. I felt very special. Chosen by him.

"Okay," said Ducky a few minutes later. "Here we are."

He had pulled into the driveway of a large house. If the lawn of the house hadn't been littered with cups and papers and things, and if the pool hadn't been full of ruined lawn furniture, I would never have guessed that this was where the party had been held. It seemed so different in the daytime. And in the quiet, with no party guests.

Ducky had said that no one was at home, and it certainly looked that way — a sleepy house, the windows closed, the garage door pulled down. Not a sign of life.

"Okay," said Sunny. "I might as well start looking by those bushes."

She pointed to the scene of her barf fest.

Ducky and I spread out in other directions. But I hadn't gone far when I thought I heard a door open. I whirled around — just in time to see a woman say to Sunny, "Is this what you're looking for?"

Sure enough, the woman had come through the front door of the house, the house that looked unoccupied. I froze, twisted around with one arm in front of me and the other at my side.

The woman was holding an object out toward Sunny. Even at a distance I recognized it as Sunny's wallet. Her wallet is neon pink plastic, hard not to see. Which was probably why the woman had already found it.

"Um, yes," said Sunny in a small voice, reaching for the wallet.

"Okay. Come here, then. All three of you."

I glanced at Ducky, who was crawling out from under a bush.

Ducky and I approached the woman. I thought she looked familiar.

I thought she was a teacher at Vista.

She was. "Hi, Ms. Krueger," said Ducky sheepishly.

"Hello, Christopher."

"Ms. Krueger, honestly we did not know

this was your house," said Ducky. "Not before the party, and not now. I mean, I guess you know that some of the other kids knew — "

My mouth dropped open. "What?"

" — but I didn't. And Dawn and Sunny certainly didn't."

"Who thought up this prank?" Ms. Krueger asked Ducky.

"I'm not sure. All I knew was that the party was going to be held at a house where no one was home this weekend."

"As if that weren't bad enough," said Ms. Krueger.

Sunny and I were looking from Ducky to Ms. Krueger like we were at a tennis match. I had no idea what they were talking about.

"_What_ are you talking about?" Sunny blurted out.

"I'll explain in the car," Ducky replied. He paused. Then he shrugged. "Well, we got what we came for. Come on, you guys."

"Not so fast," said Ms. Krueger. "All right. Christopher McCrae and Sunny

Winslow, I know you two were here last night." (Ms. Krueger must have looked in Sunny's wallet.) She turned to me. "And your name would be?"

I considered giving her a fake name, but I couldn't do that to Sunny and Ducky. If they were going to get into trouble, then I would get into trouble with them.

I sighed. "Dawn Schafer," I told her.

"Dawn Schafer," she repeated. She looked at each of us in turn. "Do your parents know where you were last night?" I decided she had sort of a nice face, especially for someone who was probably in the process of ruining my life. It was narrow, lightly freckled, with gentle brown eyes. Everything about her seemed soft, even when she was asking hard questions.

"Not technically," I replied.

Ms. Krueger looked like she was about to say something else, but before she could, Sunny cried, "Are you going to press charges?"

"Press ... charges?" Ms. Krueger swallowed back a smile. "It doesn't quite work like that. I'm not sure what I'm going to do. In the meantime, please keep this in mind: My husband and I were away for the weekend on a much-deserved and long-awaited minivacation. We were phoned in the middle of the night by the police saying that our yard had been trashed and we might want to return right away, which we did. Now we get to spend the remainder of our vacation cleaning up _this_." She waved her arm around, indicating the sea of mud, litter, and broken furniture.

"Ms. Krueger, we didn't know. We really didn't!" I cried. "We got these invitations and we thought the party was going to be at the house belonging to whoever sent the invitations. We didn't know <u>no</u> one would be there — or that it was <u>your</u> house."

"I know you didn't. It wasn't your fault. ...You I'm not so sure about," she said to Ducky.

A few minutes later, Ms. Krueger let us go. "But this isn't over yet," she called after us.

"I didn't think so," muttered Sunny.

Tuesday afternoon 10/7

Having survived today (miraculously, it seems), I can finish writing about the weekend more calmly. And so the story continues. . . .

The second Sunny and I were settled into Ducky's car, Sunny looked in her wallet, which wasn't missing a thing. Then we bombarded Ducky with questions.

"_You_ knew the party was going to be held at an empty house?" I asked him.

"_It_ was a prank?" said Sunny.

"Are you _sure_ you didn't know this was Ms. Krueger's house?" I said.

Ducky answered that last question first. "No. I honestly didn't know this was Ms. Krueger's house. I wouldn't have come over here if _I'd_ known." When Sunny and I didn't say anything, Ducky added even more seriously, "The party was a prank thought up by the upperclassmen. It was their way of hazing the eighth-graders. They planned this mysterious party and they decided to hold it at Ms. Krueger's house because they knew she wouldn't be home this weekend. They served liquor at the party, and they waited until things got just out of control enough, and then they called the cops. I'm not sure who made the call, but the plan was for the caller to say he was a neighbor and complain about the noise or something. Then all the upperclassmen left. The only kids who got caught were a bunch of eighth-graders. But I didn't know half of this until I got to the party."

Sunny slumped in her seat. "Oh, man."

"We got tricked," I added glumly.

"Our parents are going to know what we did last night," said Sunny. "That's all my mom needs right now."

Ducky glanced at Sunny in the rearview mirror, but all he said was, "I don't know. Ms. Krueger's okay. Let's just wait and see what happens."

"Easy for you to say. If you get in trouble, your parents won't hear about it for months. And what are they going to do from Ghana, anyway?" muttered Sunny.

The rest of the ride was pretty quiet. At last Ducky pulled up in front of my house, and Sunny and I climbed out. "See you tomorrow!" called Ducky. "Everything's going to be okay. Really."

"'Bye!" I called back.

Sunny was halfway across the lawn on her way to her house when suddenly I remembered something. "Hey, Sunny!" I yelled. "Yesterday I promised Jill I'd go back to the mall with her. I better keep the promise. You don't want to come with us, do you?"

Sunny shook her head. "Nah. Jill's kind of driving me crazy right now. Besides, I should go visit my mom."

"Okay. See you later."

Well, there's nothing like a bad secret to cause a little resentment. The moment I walked through the front door and saw Carol, I thought about the baby and all the questions I wasn't allowed to ask anyone. Carol was dressed in tennis whites and eating an ice cream cone. Not exactly the picture of a pregnant woman.

I answered Carol's questions about the sleepover with "Yeah" and "Uh-huh" and "Nope" and other things grown-ups hate.

Then I called Jill and arranged to meet her at The Bear Necessities in half an hour. And then I made my great escape. I told Carol I'd be back in time for dinner.

At the mall, Jill moped around The Bear Necessities, poking at stickers, glancing at pencils and erasers and teddy bears and ponies. Finally I said to her, "Come on. Let's go to Starburst's. Let's get a soda or an iced tea or something. You don't really want to shop. Do you?"

Jill shook her head. I could see tears in her eyes. She tossed a fuzzy bear pin back into a basket. Then she led the way out of the store.

At Starburst's I ordered an iced tea for me and a lemonade for Jill.

"I'm really sorry about the party," I said finally.

"Which one?"

"Both. Yours, for ruining it. And the other one, for going to it."

"It's okay."

"No, it isn't. We shouldn't have gone."

Jill was quiet for a moment. Then she

said softly, "You could have gotten killed last night."

That seemed like an exaggeration. But not much of one.

"Walking all the way over there in the middle of the night? You could have been murdered."

"You're right."

"Dawn, you're my friend. I care about you. I don't want anything to happen to you. Anything bad, I mean."

"I know," I said again. I felt a little like I was having a conversation with Dad or Carol. The conversation in which the parent says (as he or she sets some limit or takes away some privilege), "I'm not doing this to be mean, I'm doing it because I love you." Still, it made me feel more kindly toward Jill. After what we had done to her last night, she still cared about us. About me, anyway.

Jill was looking at me solemnly. She frowned slightly. "Dawn? Is something going on with you? Something I don't know about?"

I sighed. "Oh, kind of everything. You

know — school, Sunny's mom, all these changes. A lot."

Jill was still frowning. "No, I don't mean that. You've seemed different in the last few days."

Suddenly I remembered one of the many reasons Jill and I had been such good friends. Because Jill is sensitive. She could practically read my mind. It was uncanny, but I liked it.

"Well . . ." I began.

"You can tell me," said Jill.

"All right, but it's a _huge_ secret. You cannot tell a soul, and I mean not one single solitary soul. Because I promised Carol _I_ would not tell anyone this secret."

"Okay." Jill was still as solemn as a cat.

"Carol," I said, "is pregnant."

Jill's eyes widened. Her mouth opened. Then she grinned.

"But," I hurried on, "somehow it's not a good thing." I tried to describe Carol's reaction, how she hadn't told Dad and seemed all nervous — and frankly not very pregnant.

Jill frowned again. "Wow. That is strange," she said.

"I don't like the way Carol is handling things," I went on. "Not telling Dad, making me keep it a secret. Anyway, remember — Carol told me this in confidence."

"Well, your secret is safe with me." Jill pretended to zip her lips together, then to lock them and throw away the key. Very third grade but somehow confidence inspiring. When we left Starburst's I felt closer to Jill than I'd felt in a long time. I still thought that I was outgrowing her, but I wanted to be her friend anyway.

Tuesday night 10/7

So. Those are — finally — all the events of the weekend. Now when I explain what happened yesterday and today, everything will make sense. Here's one of the many good things about keeping these journals: When you read about the bad stuff, you remember how horrible everything seemed. Then you keep reading — the next entry and the next entry and the next and the next — and you see that you survived. That life goes on. Not only that, but the bad things seem less bad. And they seem that way very quickly. Maybe it's good that our feelings don't have the long, accurate memories our brains have. I guess this is a self-protection device, like the spots on a fawn. Or maybe it's healing for our minds. Whatever.

Anyway, here it is only Tuesday, and already Saturday, Sunday, and Monday don't seem so bad.

Yesterday morning (Monday) us stupid eighth-graders had to show our faces at school, had to look into the eyes of all those upperclassmen who didn't really like us at all, who probably didn't want us in their building (or their lives), who had used our eagerness to join the big leagues to put us right back in our unenviable little places. I wanted to walk into school with my head

hanging, wearing sunglasses. But Sunny
wouldn't let me do the first, and we aren't
allowed to do the second.

I realized something interesting the
moment Sunny and Maggie and I did enter
our building: It was the upperclassmen who
couldn't look at us. They were in trouble too.

"They set us up and called the police
on us," Maggie said.

I felt a tap on my shoulder and turned
around. Ducky was standing behind us.

"Hey," he greeted us.

"Hi!" we said.

"Have you heard?" Ducky went on.
"There's big trouble."

That much I knew. The mood certainly
was tense.

"What kind of trouble?" I asked. "I
mean, specifically."

Ducky shrugged. "I'm not sure. Just a
lot of rumors right now. But heads are
going to roll." Ducky pulled something out
of his shirt pocket. "Gum?" he said,
holding it out to us. Sunny took a piece, and
Ducky said, "The administration has figured
out exactly what happened. The kids who

organized the party are in deep trouble with their parents."

"What about the kids the police picked up at the party?" Sunny asked.

"They're in equally deep trouble."

"Hey, you guys."

I turned around to find Amalia hurrying toward us.

"Amalia! How are you?" I cried.

"What happened after we dropped you off?" asked Sunny.

"I got busted. Mom and Dad were waiting for me in their bedroom. They'd already found out I hadn't been baby-sitting. I'm grounded for a month. Except for school, of course," said Amalia.

"Whoa," I said.

"Wow," said Ducky.

During homeroom that morning, Mr. Dean made an announcement. He sounded mad. This was the entire announcement: "Will all eighth-, ninth-, tenth-, eleventh-, and twelfth-graders report to the auditorium at ten o'clock sharp tomorrow morning, please. Do not miss the assembly. No excuses accepted."

That was it. The entire announcement.

I glanced at Tray Farmer. Our eyes exchanged a look. It meant, Uh-oh.

When homeroom ended, I hurried into the hallway. I was making my way to my next class when I nearly ran into Ms. Krueger.

"Oh! Um, hi," I said.

"Hi, Dawn. I've been looking for you. Sunny and Christopher too. I wanted to tell the three of you — in person — to meet me in my office before tomorrow's assembly. Quarter to ten, please. I'll see you then."

"Oh, okay. I mean, fine. I mean, see you then," I babbled as Ms. Krueger hurried away. "Quarter to ten!" I called after her.

I was a nervous wreck by lunchtime. "Sunny, did Ms. Krueger find you this morning?" I asked her.

"Yes," said Sunny hotly. "And she can't do anything about us. We didn't break the law or anything. We were just looking for my wallet."

"On _her_ private property," I pointed out. "The scene of a wild party she did not give us permission to have."

"I know, I know, I know," muttered Sunny.

Sunny, Maggie, Jill, and I sat at our usual table in the cafeteria. The four of us looked sick. Sick with fear. Even Jill, because she knew that if our parents ever learned that some of us had been at the party, she would be in Big Trouble for covering for us.

"Let's hang out together this afternoon," I said, needing moral support.

"I can't," said Sunny. "I promised Mom I'd spend some time with her at the hospital. I told her I'd do her nails."

"I can't either," said Maggie. "That big English assignment is due on Wednesday. I didn't work on it at all over the weekend."

"I'll hang out with you, Dawn," said Jill loyally.

"Okay. You want to come over?"

"Will Mrs. Bruen let us bake cookies?"

"Sure, unless she's in the middle of making dinner."

And that was how Jill wound up at my house yesterday afternoon and nearly ruined my life.

Bedtime, Tuesday night 10/7

I swear, just when things look their bleakest (which is how they still looked yesterday), something comes along and makes them look totally black. This time the something was Jill. What gets into her?

Jill and I walked to my house after school yesterday. We were not in tip-top shape. We were exhausted (well, I was), and the assembly was hanging over our heads like a storm cloud.

"What do you think Mr. Dean is going to say tomorrow?" asked Jill.

"I can't imagine," I replied. Jill looked at me sideways, trying to tell whether I was being sarcastic. "I mean, I really can't," I added quickly. "It depends on how much he knows, I guess, and on how big a stink he wants to make of it. After all, this doesn't look very good for Vista."

Jill brightened. "That's true."

"But still," I said.

"Yeah."

When we reached my house, Mrs. Bruen

was hanging clothes on the line in the backyard. She said she didn't need the kitchen for awhile, and that Jill and I could use it.

"We'll clean up!" Jill called over her shoulder as we ran inside.

We found Carol sitting at the kitchen table.

"Hi," I said. "How come you're home from work?" It was only then that I realized her car was parked in the driveway.

"I decided to work at home this afternoon," she told us.

"Do you mind if we make cookies?" I asked her.

"Nope. Go ahead. I'll be in the den."

Jill and I set to work mixing and stirring.

"I wonder what it feels like to be grounded," Jill said after awhile.

"Grounded? What do you mean? Why?"

"Well, I've never been grounded. But if my mom finds out about the party, and that I lied —"

"Jill! Shh!" I hissed. "Do you want Carol to hear us?"

Jill lowered her voice. "I guess if we all get grounded it won't be so bad. Of course, we wouldn't have to worry about this in the first place if you guys hadn't snuck out — "

"Jill!" I cried again. "Shh. SHH! Carol is coming."

At that moment Carol entered the kitchen. She was carrying a box. It was labeled PRO-MAX 220 FAX MACHINE.

"A fax machine!" Jill leaped to her feet. "Carol, you shouldn't be carrying that. Not in your condition. It's too heavy. Here, let me." Jill reached for the box.

She realized too late what she had said. She dropped her arms.

Carol looked at me, eyes flashing. Jill looked at me nervously. I looked back at both of them. Finally I said, "Good one, Jill."

"I'm sorry," she whispered.

Carol set the box on the table. "Well, I thought I could trust you, Dawn," was all she said. Then she left the room.

"You can't keep your mouth shut, can you?" I said to Jill. "What is it with you? Don't you ever think? I mean, think like an adult?"

"I'm sorry, Dawn," Jill said again. "I was just trying to help. I didn't want Carol to hurt herself. Or the baby."

"Jill, I told you the baby was like the biggest secret in the world. I told you not to tell a soul. I told you that _I_ wasn't supposed to have told a soul. And then you let the secret out — to _Carol_ of all people. Who else did you tell?"

"No one. I swear." Jill was wringing her hands. "But if it was such a big secret, why _did_ you tell me?"

"I don't know. I guess it's my fault. I should have known I couldn't trust you with a secret." I turned away from Jill. "What a baby," I muttered.

Jill burst into tears. She didn't say anything, though. Not to me. She just crossed the kitchen, picked up the phone, called her mother, and asked her to come pick her up.

I was so mad that I went to my room without a word. Jill sat alone on our front stoop until her mother arrived.

Wednesday morning 10/8

I stayed in my room for quite awhile. I thought about Jill and Carol and the baby and Dad. Finally I went to the den and apologized to Carol. Carol apologized back. It was all very polite. Too polite. I knew Carol was still disappointed in me.

Well, guess what. I was disappointed in Carol. The secret made no sense to me. It was ridiculous that Dad didn't know the news yet. He was going to be a <u>father</u> again. But the only people who knew that were Carol and me. And Jill.

That night, Dad called. Jeff spoke to him first. He told him an elephant joke and complained about his soccer coach. Then I got on the phone and told Dad about Sunny and Mrs. Winslow and my homework and lots of other things — but not that he was soon going to have another son or daughter. When I handed the phone to Carol, I covered the mouthpiece and said, "It's Dad. He called to find out how his children are." I paused. "His <u>children</u>."

"All <u>right</u>," said Carol irritably.

As I left Carol's bedroom, I heard her say, "Hi, Jack. It's me. I'm glad you called. I want to talk to you."

I almost cried "Yess!" I was planning to listen in on the rest of the conversation, but Carol closed her door then. By the time I was ready for bed, she hadn't opened it.

Wednesday 10/8, in study hall

Promptly at 9:45 yesterday morning, Sunny and Ducky and I met outside Ms. Krueger's office. I was so nervous that my hands were shaking. Sunny looked pale. Ducky seemed subdued.

Ms. Krueger had lined up three chairs across from her desk. She sat behind her desk and we sat in the chairs, fidgeting, biting our lips, playing with our hair, and jiggling our feet.

"Calm down, kids," said Ms. Krueger pleasantly. "Look, the teachers have been investigating the party for three days now. We know you weren't responsible for it. You just happened to get caught. And so you win a private lecture."

My jiggling foot slowed down from eighty miles an hour to thirty.

"Let's start with this," Ms. Krueger went on. "How did you kids get to the party?" She peered at us over her glasses.

"I drove," said Ducky.

"Um, we walked," Sunny said, pointing first to herself, then to me.

"Two girls? Alone? After dark?"

"Well . . . yes," I said.

"Do you have any idea what that might have led to?"

"I —" said Sunny.

"Um —" I said.

"I guess it could have been dangerous," said Sunny finally.

"That's putting it mildly," said Ms. Krueger. "Without unduly scaring you," she continued, "you could have been robbed, kidnapped, or attacked. You could have been hit by a car, especially out on the country roads where there are no sidewalks. You would have been a lovely target for a drunk driver. Did you think about that?"

"No," Sunny and I admitted.

"Did you tell anyone where you were going?"

"Jill sort of knew. I mean, she had the address," said Sunny.

"Jill's our friend," I added, purposely not telling Ms. Krueger Jill's last name. (I noticed that Ms. Krueger didn't ask for her last name, which I appreciated.) "She refused to go to the party."

"Smart girl," replied Ms. Krueger. "Well, at least someone 'sort of' knew where you girls were going to be. What about you?" she asked Ducky.

"No one exactly knew," Ducky admitted.

"Great," said Ms. Krueger. "So if you hadn't come home on Saturday night, your brother wouldn't have discovered this until Sunday morning, and he would have had no idea where to start looking for you. Is that right?"

"Yeah."

"Okay. Now, about the drinking. Sunny, on Sunday morning you looked to me like a young woman with a hangover." (Sunny blushed but didn't say anything.) "I'm not going to go into _all_ the dangers of drinking too much. I just want to make sure that you know about a condition called alcohol poisoning. It can easily happen when you're drinking a lot. And it can lead quickly to death." (Sunny's eyes widened and her chin trembled, but still she said nothing.) "Now let's see," Ms. Krueger went on. "What else? I imagine kids at the party were smoking, but you probably know about the dangers of smoking. Also, the party was held at a house that was unoccupied. I'm sure you've thought about how you would have summoned help, if it were needed, when you couldn't get to a phone."

"Ms. Krueger?" said Ducky then. "The party was really stupid. We know that now. We did a lot of stupid things that night."

"We _didn't_ know," said Sunny defiantly, "that the upperclassmen were going to play a trick on us, though. I mean, maybe Ducky knew, but Dawn and I didn't. That wasn't our fault. We didn't know we were going to an empty house."

"Were the upperclassmen responsible for

your choosing to get drunk? Or choosing to walk to the party alone in the middle of the night?" Ms. Krueger asked Sunny, raising an eyebrow.

"No."

"Look, kids, I'm just trying to point out how dangerous Saturday night could have been for you. The bottom line is that you're not going to get in trouble —"

"We're not?" Sunny asked.

"No, you're not. You did get tricked. And you didn't think. And you are very lucky that nothing more than a hangover happened. But you are not going to get punished. At least not individually. And not this time."

"Thank you," I said.

"What does 'not this time' mean?" Sunny asked suspiciously.

"It means if I hear about this sort of thing in the future, I'm going to come down hard on you three. I'll be in touch with your parents — even yours, Christopher — so fast your heads will spin. Is that understood?"

Yes, it was understood. And at that

moment I decided Ms. Krueger was a very cool adult. I understood exactly what she was doing ... scaring us (it worked), giving us one warning (I knew it truly was exactly one warning), then letting us off the hook.

I hope I get Ms. Krueger for a teacher one day.

When Ms. Krueger let Sunny and Ducky and me go, we exploded into the hall.

"Head directly for the assembly," Ms. Krueger called after us.

"Okay!" I called back.

"Whoa," exclaimed Ducky.

"Oh, man," said Sunny, shaking her head.

"What?" I asked.

"She's such a dork."

"Who? Ms. Krueger?" asked Ducky.

"Who else?" said Sunny.

"She let us off the hook," I said incredulously. "She could have called our parents, you know. Instead of talking to us, she could have sat there and dialed our parents while we watched."

"I know. But scaring us with all that

stuff about drinking and smoking and walking around at night. I feel so stupid."

"I think that was the point," said Ducky.

Wednesday afternoon 10/8

The assembly wasn't what I had expected. Since all the teachers knew that the mean upperclassmen had tricked us poor eighth-graders, I had come to believe that the principal or someone would haul the kids who had dreamed up the party onto the stage and lecture them publicly, then ask them to apologize to us and especially to the kids who were picked up by the police. That wasn't exactly what happened.

This is what happened:

Sunny and Ducky and I found Maggie and Amalia at the entrance to the auditorium. They were waiting for us while kids streamed by and scrambled for seats inside. I noticed that Jill was hanging around, several feet away from Maggie and Amalia, maybe hoping to sit with Maggie. But when she saw Sunny and Ducky, she backed off, and when she saw me, she reddened, then hurried into the auditorium alone. Good, I thought.

"What happened? What happened?" Maggie asked as soon as she saw us. She was bouncing up and down.

"It wasn't so bad," I said. Then Ducky and Sunny and I told her and Amalia about our visit with Ms. Krueger.

Afterward, we found seats in the auditorium. We couldn't get five together, exactly, but we found two together in one row, with three together behind them. Then I sat back and waited for the upperclassmen — the ones who had dreamed up the party — to get into trouble.

What happened instead was that Mr. Dean, flanked by the new headmistress of Vista and one of the guidance counselors, gave everyone a big talk about responsibility, respect, and trust. The kids who'd been picked up at the party by the police, we found out, had been let off with warnings.

The kids who had given the party had also received warnings, apparently, but not from the police, just from Mr. Dean. The assembly was like a mass version of what Sunny and Ducky and I had just been through with Ms. Krueger. Except for Mr. Dean's last words.

"You are all — every last one of you — as of right now, considered on probation. Upperclassmen, if I hear about any more hazing of the eighth-graders, those of you responsible for the hazing will be suspended immediately."

Yess! I thought.

"And all of you — this includes the eighth-graders — if I hear of any of you drinking, lying to your parents, sneaking out, defacing property, trespassing ..." (as Mr. Dean's list went on, I sank a bit in my seat), "then you will be suspended immediately. I am deeply disappointed in those of you involved with Saturday night's party. Beyond that, I'm ashamed of you. As a final note, I will tell you that the damage to Ms. Krueger's personal property totaled approximately two thousand dollars.

Ms. Krueger is going to be recompensed for it — with your class funds. That comes to just under four hundred dollars per class. By the way, that leaves the ninth-graders and the eleventh-graders with nothing. In fact, each of these classes will still owe Ms. Krueger about seventy-five dollars. You can pay her back what you owe her as soon as you've earned the money with your next class fund-raiser. Neither of these classes, however, will have enough money at the end of the year for their usual trip. All right. This assembly is hereby dismissed."

My mouth hung open. So did just about everyone else's. Around me kids were complaining, groaning, exclaiming.

You know what? I didn't expect it. But I know we deserved it.

At first no one moved. Then, slowly, kids began to stand up (looking stunned) and make their way to the auditorium doors. Maggie, Sunny, Ducky, Amalia, and I joined them.

"Oh, _man_," said Sunny, which she says a lot these days.

"Whoa," added Amalia.

"I can't believe they're taking the money out of our class funds," said Maggie as we made our way to the aisle.

"We worked hard for that money," said Ducky.

"I can't believe we did two thousand dollars' worth of damage to Ms. Krueger's yard," I said. "I mean, I can believe it — we saw all the stuff in the pool and the ruined lawn and everything. I just can't believe we did it." I pictured the ruined yard. I felt horrible. Then I began to get an idea.

"No class trip for the ninth-graders and the eleventh-graders," said Sunny. "That really rots."

"The rest of us aren't going to have money for anything but a class trip," I pointed out. We headed into the hall. But my mind wasn't really on class trips. It was on my idea.

"Hey, here comes Justin!" Sunny suddenly whispered to Maggie.

Sure enough, Justin Randall and two other guys brushed past us. Justin nodded at us, said hi to Maggie, and eyed her (another admiring look, I might add). Then the boys hustled off.

And _that_ was when I caught sight of Mandy and her friends. "Uh-oh," I said under my breath.

"What?" asked Amalia.

Before I could answer her, Mandy planted herself in front of Maggie and said, "So. Did you find your wallet?"

Sunny narrowed her eyes. "How did you know anything about a wallet? And it was _my_ wallet, by the way."

Mandy looked disappointed at first, and then confused, but just for a moment. "Oh. Was it yours? You little kids are so hard to tell apart."

"_I can't believe you planted my wallet_—" Sunny started to say at the same time Amalia said, "Justin Randall doesn't think so."

Once again, I wanted to smirk but didn't. Mandy scared me. I could tell she scared the others too. Amalia already looked sorry that she'd made that remark. But remembering what Mr. Dean had said about the upperclassmen and hazing, I figured

Mandy wasn't going to do anything horrible to us. At least not right now.

Wednesday night 10/8

I was right. Mandy didn't do anything horrible. She let the matter drop. She and her friends turned and walked away.

I looked at Maggie and Amalia and Ducky and Sunny. I smiled uncomfortably.

Maggie and Amalia and Sunny smiled back at me.

But Ducky was staring after Mandy and her friends, an odd look on his face.

"What is it?" I asked him. "What's wrong?"

Ducky shook his head slightly. Then he said, "I know them better than you do. That's all." He frowned.

"What's that supposed to mean?" asked Maggie.

"Nothing," replied Ducky. "Come on. We don't want to be late for class."

Ducky turned on his great grin. He extended his elbows to Amalia and me. We took them. Behind us, Maggie and Sunny linked arms. We headed for our classes. Our big adventure was over.

Thursday 10/9

Well, the adventure was over, but the day wasn't. There was more to come, and it was directly related to the party and the weekend. _Related_ only, though. When I think about what happened on Tuesday afternoon, I don't entirely understand it. Maybe I never will. People, friends, relationships . . . they are very confusing things.

Actually, there are a lot of things I don't understand. Like, why _couldn't_ Carol tell Dad the news about the baby over the phone? I mean, eventually she did tell him over the phone, but why did she think she couldn't at first? And why are Mandy and her friends so mean to me and my friends? It must be more than the swimming pool and Justin Randall and the locker mix-up. The swimming pool was an accident, Justin didn't come along until later (after

Mandy had already decided she hated me),
and most people would have been
understanding about the locker mix-up. They
would simply have said, "Excuse me, this
is _my_ locker. Yours is in the next hallway."
Why did Mandy get so mad? I know I
broke her mirror, but still ...

There are some nice things I don't
understand either. Why do most people go
along with their same old group of friends
and then, bang, suddenly they have some
new ones? I started out last weekend with
Sunny, Maggie, and Jill, and by Sunday I
had two new friends — Ducky and Amalia.
I feel like I've known them all my life,
when really I've known them less than a
week. It's great. _And_ it's another mystery.

Circles of friends widen and narrow,
widen and narrow. My circle widened over
the weekend. Then, on Tuesday, it narrowed.

I lost Jill.

It was my own fault. Mostly.

You know what? I ran into a lot of
trouble over the weekend, and before (with
Mandy), and after (with Ms. Krueger and
the assembly and everything). But writing

about all those things rolled up into one
enormous, tangled ball is nowhere near as
painful as writing about Jill. I'm going to
do it, though. Write about her, I mean. Well,
about us. Because I know that afterward
I'll feel better.

First, I need to compose myself.

Okay. Here goes.

After the assembly on Tuesday, life at
Vista seemed to return to normal. A lot of
kids had gotten in trouble, but at least we
knew where we stood. No more surprises. The
party was behind us. Not forgotten, but over.
We could get on with things. And us eighth—
graders could get on with things without
worrying about hazing. Plus, I was still
thinking about my idea, and I liked it a lot.
I planned to organize groups of kids to
go to Ms. Krueger's over the next few weeks
and fix up the lawn, maybe plant some new
stuff in the gardens. We could even find a
way to raise some more money to buy plants
and things. I knew kids would like the
idea.

Life went on. We went to our morning
classes. I ate lunch in the cafeteria with

Sunny, Ducky, Maggie, and Amalia. Jill was sitting at a table with Peg and some other friends of hers. Not usual, but not exactly unusual, either. When lunch was over, we went to our afternoon classes. And after the final bell rang, we went to our lockers.

I was just closing the door to mine, juggling books, a jacket, an umbrella, and a bag full of dirty gym clothes, when I sensed someone standing directly behind me. Mandy, I thought, and whirled around.

But I found myself facing Jill.

"Dawn," she said. "Hi. I was — I wanted to talk to you."

I let out a breath. "Me too," I said.

"You did?"

"Yup."

"You go first."

"Well," I began, now feeling slightly unprepared.

"Did you want to say you're sorry? Because that's what I wanted to say."

"Um, I guess — yeah, that's what I wanted to say. I'm sorry I yelled at you. I shouldn't have gotten so mad."

"And I'm sorry I opened my mouth.

What's that phrase? Open mouth, insert foot?" (This happens to be a phrase I can't stand.) "Well, that's what I did. I opened mouth and inserted foot. I do that sometimes."

Even though I hate that phrase I smiled at Jill. "That's okay." I felt relieved to be talking to her again. We hadn't spoken since our fight on Monday. One whole day.

"So," said Jill as we began to walk down the hallway, "what happened with Ms. Krueger? Anything?"

I told Jill about the meeting in Ms. Krueger's office with Sunny and Ducky. "Mostly, we just got a lecture."

"A lecture?" Jill looked vaguely disappointed.

"Yeah. You know. She tried to scare us."

"What do you mean?"

"She told Sunny about alcohol poisoning, and she pointed out all the dangers of walking around late at night, and going out without telling anyone where you are. That kind of thing."

Jill just stared at me.

"What?" I said.

"That's all?"

"Well . . . yeah. Why?"

"Oh, I don't know. It seems to me that a lot of kids who didn't do anything wrong — like me — got into trouble for what you guys did. Plus, none of you guys got into very much trouble for what you did do on Saturday."

"Did you <u>want</u> us to get into trouble?"

"Well . . ." Jill said slowly, not quite looking at me. She stopped walking.

"Oh, that's nice, Jill," I said. "That is very nice."

"Nice? You call ditching your friends nice?"

"No. I don't call it nice. But I already apologized to you for that. What do you want, Jill? What do you want from me?"

"I want — I want —" Jill stammered.

"Whatever it is, I'm not sure I can give it to you."

"But it's not fair," said Jill.

"What's not fair?"

"You guys did something wrong and you're hardly getting into trouble."

"Jill, what is your problem? We have already been through that. Look, things are not always equal. They're not always fair or even. They're not always black-and-white. Maybe we try to make them that way when we're kids, but when we get older we see that the world just isn't that way, no matter how much we'd like it to be. You have to let go of that, Jill. Quit being such a b —. Just grow up."

"Hey, Dawn?"

I turned around at the sound of Sunny's voice. She was calling to me from halfway down the hall. "Yeah?" I said.

"Maggie's waiting outside. Are you coming?"

"I'll — I'll be right there. You go ahead."

Sunny left, and I turned back to Jill.

When I looked at Jill's face I knew that our friendship was over. Something had changed. Jill had changed. I had changed. Whatever. Our lives had veered off in different directions, and we simply were no longer friends.

"I have to go," I said to Jill.

"Yeah. Me too."

And that was that. I walked away. I knew Jill was standing where I'd left her. "I'm sorry," I called over my shoulder. And I _was_ sorry. Just not sorry enough to work things out with her.

Ann M. Martin

About the Author

ANN MATTHEWS MARTIN was born on August 12, 1955. She grew up in Princeton, NJ, with her parents and her younger sister, Jane.

Although Ann used to be a teacher and then an editor of children's books, she's now a full-time writer. She gets the ideas for her books from many different places. Some are based on personal experiences. Others are based on childhood memories and feelings. Many are written about contemporary problems or events.

All of Ann's characters are made up. But some of her characters are based on real people. Sometimes Ann names her characters after people she knows, other times she chooses names she likes.

In addition to California Diaries, Ann Martin has written many other books, including the Baby-sitters Club series. She has written twelve novels for young people, including *Missing Since Monday*, *With You or Without You*, *Slam Book*, and *Just a Summer Romance*.

Ann M. Martin does not live in California, though she does visit frequently. She lives in New York with her cats, Gussie and Woody. Her hobbies are reading, sewing, and needlework — especially making clothes for children.

LOOK FOR #2

Sunny

I DO NOT NEED THIS.

IF I KEEP MY CHIN UP AND ACT HAPPY, I FEEL GUILTY. IF I WORRY TOO MUCH, I LOSE SLEEP.

I NEED TO GET AWAY, DO SOMETHING FUN. BUT CAN I? NO. OUR BIG TRIP TO LAKE TAHOE, WHICH WE PLANNED FOR MONTHS? POSTPONED WHEN MOM GOT SICK. MY BIG BLOWOUT PARTY AT OUR HOUSE FOR ALL MY FRIENDS? CANCELED.

"WE HAVE TO PUT THINGS ON HOLD," DAD SAYS, "UNTIL WE KNOW MORE ABOUT MOM. JUST BE PATIENT."

WELL, THAT'S EASY FOR HIM TO SAY. HE HAS THE STORE. IT'S HIS LIFE.

BUT HELLO, WHAT ABOUT MY LIFE? I'M SUPPOSED TO HAVE ONE TOO.

I FEEL AS IF SOMEONE IS STANDING OVER ME
WITH A REMOTE, PRESSING THE PAUSE BUTTON.

I KEEP WAITING FOR THINGS TO GET BACK TO
NORMAL. BUT SOMETIMES I THINK THAT'S A STUPID
IDEA. I DON'T KNOW WHAT NORMAL IS ANYMORE.
WHEN I THINK OF THE FUTURE, MY MIND TURNS
INTO SOUP. WILL DAD AND I MOVE TO A SMALLER
HOUSE? WILL HE TOTALLY FREAK OUT? WILL HE
START DATING? WILL I HAVE TO TAKE A JOB IN
HIS STORE, OR LEARN TO DO THE BILLS AND MAKE
DINNERS THE WAY MOM DOES?

HONESTLY, SOMETIMES I WISH MOM WOULD JUST
GO AHEAD AND DIE SO WE CAN GET ON WITH
EVERYTHING.

OH MY LORD.

I WROTE THAT. I REALLY DID.

From Best-selling Author
ANN M. MARTIN

Who knew life was gonna be this hard?

California Diaries

Everything's happening...
and everyone's changing.
Sometimes it seems like life is
moving way too fast for Dawn
Schafer and her California
friends. Read their diaries and
let them share their most
intimate thoughts, fears, dreams,
and secrets with you!

Look for Book #1: DAWN and Book #2: SUNNY
Available in bookstores everywhere.

CDB397

YOU READ THE BOOKS. NOW GET AWAY FROM IT ALL.

Enter the

California

Diaries

Getaway Sweepstakes

GRAND PRIZE: A California Getaway!
Now you and your friend can take off together to write your *own* California diary.

WIN A TRIP TO CALIFORNIA!

100 RUNNERS UP:
A signed copy of California Diaries Book #3: Maggie!

....

YES! Enter me in the California Diaries Getaway Sweepstakes

Name _____

Address _____

City _____ State _____ Zip _____

Send entry form to: California Diaries Getaway Sweepstakes, c/o Scholastic Inc., P.O. Box 7500, 2931 East McCarty Street, Jefferson City, MO 65102

■ SCHOLASTIC